The
ALLIANCE

Sarah Freese

QBS Publishing, Inc.
P.O. Box 922933
Atlanta, Georgia 30010-2933

1st printing 2010
Printed in U.S.A.
Library of Congress Control Number: 2010901529

ISBN: 978-1-891892-92-9

Book design by Craig Moonshower

For Mom and Dad.

Prologue

Thud, thud, thud, thud. The sound of perfectly synchronized feet echoes off the walls. I'm in a passageway with my back pressed against the wall. Torch lights move closer as the marching soldiers get nearer to where I, Trian, stand. There appears to be no escape. But I turn and scrabble up the wall behind me, the wall that stands between me and my fate.

I grab every outcropping and shove my feet into small cracks. Straining, I push myself to the top of the wall, only to come face to face with hell itself. The bodies of the dead are everywhere; falling out of windows, hanging from ropes, and literally lining the streets. It's insanity. Soldiers run from one skirmish to the next, their eyes clouded over with bloodlust. The remaining few huddle together, desperately hoping for salvation, but there is none. Laughing, the soldiers cut them down one by one.

I dart through the tunnels with the soldiers not far behind, making my way toward the one thing that needs to know about this massacre the most…the future.

One

Liz

My eyes scanned the darkness for one last glimpse of the truck's taillights. My dad's Ford, with both of my parents inside. I wanted them to leave, but honestly, I missed them already. I turned back to the massive expanse of brick buildings behind me, the brown-red brick giving off an eerie feeling in the cover of night.

My feet carried me slowly up the walkway. I dreaded returning to that small little room in Drayhorn. It was the typical freshman dorm room, where two beds, two desks, and my little refrigerator were crammed in so tightly there was hardly enough room to turn around. I had been so excited when we arrived at the University that morning. My freshman year of college! True freedom at last! I soon figured out that freedom was not what I had imagined.

Reality dawned on me as my parents and I carried box after box up the stairs to dorm room 46B. This was not freedom—this was major responsibility being heaped on my shoulders. Now, don't get me wrong, I'm a very responsible person. You might say I was the high school 'goody-two-shoes'. Salutatorian of my senior class, President of the Environmental Club, member of the National Honor Society, Vice President of FBLA, and a teacher's assistant in just about every class. Obviously, I knew about responsibility.

But this? College? This was overwhelming, maybe more than I could handle. Plus, my roommate was my complete opposite, even her name was beautiful and edgy. Brooke Washington—the queen of everything at Northbrook High. She was petite, blonde, and curvy, not to mention captain of the cheerleading squad, and head of the dance and gymnastics teams. Oh, and she was Northbrook's Homecoming Queen our senior year. The only thing I had to challenge her was that I had played decent soccer in high school, was president of the Mock Trial club, and had been salutatorian of my class. That was it.

We were opposites in many ways. Brooke was well known for getting around, and I don't mean that in a good way. Rumor had it she had slept with almost the entire football team, and she was always on the arm of a new boyfriend. The only boy I ever dated didn't really even qualify as a boyfriend. Her grades were average; mine were excellent. She drank (a lot); I didn't. The only similarity I could see was that we were both classic high school stereotypes: she was the popular slut and I was the bookworm.

When I got back to our room, good old 46B, I realized the full extent of my roommate's reputation. She was in bed with someone; one giant lump under the covers. It was the first day of college and she had already snagged a new guy. Totally disgusted and slightly humiliated, I lowered my head, grabbed a book off my desk and was out the door before they even noticed I was there.

"Slut," I muttered under my breath. I walked outside, thinking I would head to the library. It was only September, but in Maryland, the fall weather had already kicked in. I rubbed my arms through my light sweater and chided myself for not grabbing a jacket.

The University campus was dark as I walked toward the Chapman Library. Through the trees, its bright lights were warm and inviting in comparison to the chilly, bleak night. The library felt like a familiar place to me, a home away from home. I looked up at the dark, cloud-ridden sky and shivered again. Having grown up in a small town, I was used to a wide expanse of stars displayed overhead, so the smog-infested atmosphere of the big city was depressing.

I think when you're the new person somewhere, (in this case, college), there must be a sign over your head with a big arrow that screams 'I'm NEW here!' to everyone you see. I felt like everyone was watching me as I passed through the rows of bookshelves, attempting to find a quiet place to read. I passed "The Corner," the infamous make-out spot in the library, and the couple there glared at me as I hurried past. *Way to make a great impression*, I thought. My cousin, Kim, had attended the University of Maryland a few years back, and she had given me the scoop about several things, including that particular library corner.

I finally found a small couch in the back of the library. The lighting wasn't good; the fluorescent lights above flickered often. The person on the other side of the couch didn't even look up as I sat down on the other end, curled my long legs under me and prepared to knock out a few chapters. His wispy, black hair disguised his eyes, and his head bobbed slightly every once in awhile, which I supposed was in response to his reading material. I shrugged inwardly and opened up my own novel. I must have been really engrossed in the story because the next time I looked up, the guy wasn't there. I was alone on the couch, and the light was still flickering overhead.

I immediately did a self-check, mortified that he might have left because of me. *Teeth? check. Hair? check. Smell? check.* I was fine, but a little bewildered. I had only been there a few minutes, yet I still managed to run him off. *There's Brooke in bed with a guy after one day here, and I am running guys off without even talking to them,* I thought angrily. I chalked it up to an emergency on his part, and finished a few more chapters of my book.

The dorm was quiet when I returned. I practically tiptoed to my room, not sure if I would get in trouble for coming in late, or if anybody would even care. I turned on as little light as possible to change out of my clothes and get ready for bed. As I crawled in, I could almost make out the two lumps in the bed opposite mine, but my eyes were so tired I wasn't sure.

*   *   *

BEEP! BEEP! BEEP! My alarm went off promptly at 7:45 a.m. My first official day as a college student, and my 8:30 English class was all the way across campus from Drayhorn. It was a push, but I knew I could make it if I condensed the amount of "prep" time needed. I headed down to the community bathroom for a quick shower. A familiar groan escaped my lips when I saw the state of my hair in the steam-covered mirror. Normally softly curled, my dark hair was wild and stuck out in all directions. The tangles were clearly visible in the morning sunlight that peeked through the tiny window on the other side of the bathroom. I dragged a brush through it as best I could, secured most of it with a ponytail holder, and practiced my 'first class of college' smile. Light snoring came from under the door to my room as I made my way back down the hall. The boy was apparently gone, but Brooke was still dead asleep.

"Brooke," I called softly, not wanting to incite any of the fierce anger I already knew she could dish out. Her headphones blared in her ears, so I gently shook her shoulder. Her eyes snapped open and she turned to focus that awful stare on me.

"What is it?" she asked flatly, clearly perturbed that I had dared to wake her up.

"Class starts in 30 minutes," I said, as nicely as I could manage.

"So?"

"So…you have the same English class I do and it's all the way across campus…" I floundered, unable to finish my sentence under her icy stare.

"So that means I still have a good twenty minutes of sleep left."

"But…that leaves you only ten minutes to get there!" I spluttered, appalled at her lack of concern for the importance of the first day of classes.

"Fine. I'll just run," she said firmly, closing her eyes and replacing her earphones.

Liz

Even walking briskly, it took me a good 15 minutes to make it across campus to Baggart Hall, the English building. I was running behind thanks to my unpleasant exchange with Brooke. There was no way she was going to make it on time. I careened into the classroom, somewhat out of breath from rushing most of the way, and immediately felt the magnitude of 100 pairs of eyes on me as I made my way to the first open desk. A quick glance around the room told me I was the last person to be seated and instantly my face flushed. Mr. Fendel, the professor, breezed in and briefly introduced himself before starting into a lecture on the history of English literature in the modern world.

I snuck a peek around the room full of students, most of whom were well dressed and well outfitted with all the name-brand accessories. Me, I was still suffering from small town shock. I knew the sprawling city that surrounded the University was full of wealthy people. A handful of those people were probably far better off than my whole hometown combined. Still, I had never seen so many designer things in one place before. I stared in awe, amazed at the monstrous Louis Vuitton, Chanel, and Coach bags that overpowered the desks around me. I must have looked a little shell-shocked, because several girls stared back at me, raising their eyebrows critically as if to say, *Can I help you with something?* Embarrassed at my obvious naiveté, I quickly returned my attention to my own desk. I felt so insignificant compared to the other students in the class. No doubt they were making fun of the Vera Bradley knock off bag hanging on my seat—the one I had been so proud of before today.

Mr. Fendel was about one minute into his lecture when I saw a somewhat familiar face appear in the window of the door to the auditorium. It was Brooke peering in through the rectangular pane, and it seemed that the only one who noticed her was me.

Just play along, she mouthed through the glass. I hesitated, unsure of what to do. She took down her messy bun, pulled a pair of glasses from her bag, put on the jacket she had carried on her arm, and then carefully knocked on the door. Mr. Fendel was startled by the interruption, but walked over quickly to open it.

"I am so sorry to bother you, Professor Fendel," Brooke cooed in a exaggerated Boston accent, "but the office sent me to tell you a big package just came for you." Mr. Fendel looked skeptical.

"A big package?" he asked suspiciously.

"Seemed more mid-sized than big to me," Brooke replied evasively, carefully choosing her words, "but it must be really important, otherwise they wouldn't have sent me right over." She smiled earnestly, and Mr. Fendel began to grin. He dashed out of the classroom, calling over his shoulder to the class that he would only be a few minutes. Brooke strolled in slowly, putting her hair back up and taking off the office-like jacket to reveal a skimpy green tank top paired with a very tight pair of black jeans.

"Brooke Washington, at your service," she said in her usual, southern lilt as she walked toward an open seat in the back of the auditorium. All eyes followed her in awe and wonder, and I felt even more insignificant at this sophisticated display of personal power. I had never been good in front of a crowd, but Brooke reveled in the attention directed toward her. She had easily manipulated the professor and sidetracked the first day of class for everyone in the room. It was clear that they were all impressed. Well, all but one.

The girl next to me had not paid a bit of attention to the interruption. She was intently studying a book, her eyes scanning the words so quickly I could hardly believe she was really reading. She was dressed similarly to the boy I had sat next to in the library, mostly in blacks and grays, the only color to her wardrobe being the bright blue necklace she wore. Her hair was shoulder length and jet black. It continuously fell into her face as she read, only to be quickly tucked behind her ear once more. She was beautiful, in a dark, artistic way, nothing like the girls from my high school with their pastels and bright colors. There was something mysterious and compelling about her.

One of my fingers twirled around a strand of my own hair, as I realized I was a bit jealous of this girl, though she was in no way a threat to me. I was fascinated and couldn't help but stare, and though I think she knew I was staring, she did not look up. Slyly, I tried to stretch over enough to read the title of the book in her hands, but she carefully turned it so I could not see, disguising the maneuver with a casual arm shift.

Suddenly Mr. Fendel returned, red-faced and looking a bit confused.

"Did anyone see where that woman from the office went?" he asked, his voice taking on a shrill quality. From the back row, Brooke slowly raised her hand. Apparently, she was now unrecognizable to Mr. Fendel as the so-called office assistant, thanks to the removal of the jacket and the glasses, and her quick change of hairstyle.

"Yes, Ms...?" he began.

"Washington," she finished, her southern accent filling the room and deceiving the already flustered professor. "The assistant said she had to deliver something into town, but that she would pass by the West Campus office first. You might be able to catch her if you hurry." She smiled angelically. Professor Fendel looked frantic.

"Class dismissed!" he yelled, already halfway out the door.

The rest of the class just stared at Brooke with undisguised admiration. It wasn't even nine o'clock, yet she had definitely made the most of her first day of college. All I could do was roll my eyes and wonder what else she would come up with.

*   *   *

My other two classes went by without any more excitement, and I was disheartened to discover that Brooke was in both of them. Fuming with frustration, I stomped my way to the library, barely noticing the light rain that formed puddles on the sidewalk and dampened my clothes. Maybe a few chapters of my favorite book would improve my mood. I pretended every puddle was Brooke's face and that made me stomp even harder. I couldn't understand why no one else could see her as the manipulator she was. Guys only saw her as "The Hottie" and the girls only saw "The Next It Girl." That characterization had been true all the way through high school and now it was starting all over again in college. I grumbled as I realized that I was the only one around who knew her true self. I was the only one who knew her past and where she came from, so I was the only one who saw her clearly.

My rain boots sloshed as I stomped up the stairs to the library. Luckily I made it to the door just as the clouds opened up and it really started to pour. My hair was frizzing out of its formerly manageable ponytail, compliments of the humidity. As I reached out for the brass door handle, I almost didn't recognize my own reflection in the glass. Even more exasperated by the state of my exploding hair, I half-sprinted past the front tables and bookshelves in a mad dash to make it to the solitude of the back corner.

All of the sudden, I remembered the boy who had been there the previous night. Earlier in the day, I had prepared and even practiced a couple of conversation starters that I could use if he showed up again. I didn't put too much stock into seeing him right away, though. It was a big school, and he probably hadn't even noticed me. Funny, I usually didn't have a problem talking to people, but for the first time in my life, I wasn't sure how to begin a conversation. How do you talk to someone who probably doesn't even know you exist? Better yet, how do you talk to someone like that when you're mad as a hornet and you look like you've been run over by a bus?

I slowed down as I approached the area where my new favorite couch sat. I was a little disappointed, but not surprised, to find that the guy wasn't there. In his place sat the mysterious dark-haired girl from my English class. *This should be easier*, I thought. It was much less nerve-wracking to talk to another person of the same gender. She was still reading the book I had seen earlier in class. I recognized the brown leather binding and the strange gold markings on the inside flaps. I sat down and took a deep breath.

"Hi. What are you reading?" I asked in my nicest, greet-you-for-the-first-time voice. I waited for a response, but she said nothing. She didn't even look up, though I was certain she had heard me. After all, the couch was only meant to hold two people. It wasn't like I was far away. I cleared my throat and tried again.

"What are you reading?" I asked again, a little louder this time to be sure she heard me.

"You don't have to shout," she snipped. "I'm right here, and I'm not deaf."

Hah! I almost said out loud. Inwardly, I congratulated myself on getting her to speak, and kept the conversation going.

"Okay, so, what *are* you reading?" I asked for the third time, determined to make the conversation work. But she still didn't answer me. She merely flipped the page and continued to read quietly and quickly.

"Well, then," I said, half to myself and half at her. "What's your name?"

No reply.

"What classes are you taking besides English?"

No reply.

"Are you going to tell me what you're reading?"

No reply.

"Hello?"

No reply.

Exasperated, I put on my best authoritative voice. "Could you at least tell me if you know the boy who was sitting here yesterday? For some reason, you remind me of him, and I have some questions to ask him." I tried not to let the frustration show in my voice. Putting her finger on the page to mark her place, she slowly looked up at me with a sarcastic smile.

"He's right through there," she said, pointing to the empty wall across from her. She grinned to herself as she looked back down at her book. I stared at the space where she had pointed. The wall was perfectly blank. No door, no crack, no nothing. I stared at it intently, trying to figure out what she meant, and then turned to the surrounding bookshelves, hoping they would hold a clue. Maybe I was missing something, but I didn't understand why she would make such a strange comment. There was nothing special about a regular, stupid wall.

"By the way, I'm Liz," I said. But when I turned back toward her, she was gone, and I was alone on the couch. Again.

Liz

The week went by pretty normally after that first day—or as normally as it could. Brooke continued to have one of a few different lumps share her bed most every night. I got to know the rest of my professors for the semester and, like the good student I was, endured their boring lectures with no complaints. My course load included Sociology, Economics, Contemporary Literature, and European History. Each professor displayed different quirks, and I discovered that all of them were just a little bit insane when it came to assigning work. My European History teacher had given 150 pages of reading and several online worksheets to complete in just one night, so I was focused on tackling the mounds of work when my cell phone rang on the side of my desk.

"Hello?" I answered somewhat distractedly, still preoccupied with the huge assignment.

"Hey."

I knew immediately who was calling. It was impossible to mistake the deep, gruff voice of my brother. Twin brother, that is. Dan and I were very close, even though we had always been very different people. Dan was the jock: the kind of guy everyone loved to be around. Unlike me, he prioritized being good in sports over making good grades, and he excelled in most athletic categories. He was a big guy, so football and basketball were his favorites, but he managed to beat me in most everything else as well. I was a fairly decent soccer player, but I always struggled with balancing time for study and time for practice. Dan didn't have the same struggle. For him, sports were everything.

Near the end of the fall season of his senior year in high school, Dan was offered a full ride to play football at the University of Tennessee. What a thrill for him to be handpicked from Northbrook, our tiny hometown just north of Johnson City. Rocky Top ran in his blood, so UT had always been his dream. On the other hand, I was offered a full scholastic scholarship to the University of Maryland. Going to different schools meant that Dan and I would be separated for the first time in our lives. I had been suffering a little from missing him, and I often wondered if he felt the same separation anxiety. But then, maybe his glamorous football career had made our relationship obsolete.

"Hey Dan," I said softly, my voice wavering slightly due to my bottled up emotions. Our Northbrook classmates never discovered our close relationship, but Dan and I depended on each other

In high school, we played independent roles, mostly because Dan believed he had to maintain his social status. We ignored each other during the school day unless we were forced to interact, and even then we pretended being near each other was unbearable. But at home, when no one's social standing was at stake, we were inseparable. I helped Dan through his homework, and he kicked the soccer ball with me for hours in the backyard whenever I asked.

"So how are things at Maryland?" he asked cheerfully. "Any cute guys chasing you? Or any crazy teachers?"

"Fine, no, and yes," I laughed, my mood improving greatly just from hearing his familiar optimism. "There are also some very strange people as well."

"Strange people? Oh, do tell."

"Well, for starters, my roommate is Brooke Washington."

"Brooke Washington is your *roommate*? How come we didn't know that before you left?"

"Well, all I can figure is she must have swapped with someone so she could take advantage of my intelligence or something," I grumbled. "As usual, she's controlling and manipulative, and everyone around here is being sucked in by her fake sincerity and fake smile. She sleeps with a different guy almost every night and she's *always* late to class."

"How do you know she's always late?"

"How do I know? Because she's in every one of my classes!" I cried. "She doesn't even get out of bed until after I'm long gone. Then she strolls in right at the beginning of class!" My eyes filled with angry tears. "She's a slut and a show-off. It's just like high school all over again!" The film of water in my eyes blurred the figure that had slipped into the room as I said that last part. I blinked rapidly, trying to focus on the shape in front of me. I could feel negative energy instantly fill the room.

"Slut?" Brooke asked sweetly. "Are you calling me a slut?" Her eyes were narrowed, her face tight, and with her hands on her hips, she looked formidable, even at only 5'3".

"I…uh…um…" I sorted through excuses in my head, trying to put a together a coherent sentence, but I was completely unnerved by her angry stare. I could hear Dan talking into my ear, but at the moment, I couldn't understand a word he was saying. Brooke snatched the phone out of my hand.

"I'm sorry, she'll have to call you back," she said, her voice dripping with sarcasm and imitation sweetness. Just before she slammed the phone shut and tossed it on my bed, I could hear Dan yelling for me. "Slut?" she asked again. "I didn't know a good girl like you knew such a *dirty word*." Her velvet voice was harsh and accusing.

"I…I didn't…"

"You didn't what?" she asked tersely. "You didn't think? You didn't know? You didn't realize? Well, face the facts, *sweetie*," she said as she flipped her blonde hair, "not everybody works the way you do. The world isn't perfect. We can't all be like *you*."

"I'm not perfect," I stammered, surprised by the change of direction in her words.

"Not perfect? Are you kidding me?" She stared me down. "You're the definition of perfect. You're smart, teachers love you, and you're pretty, in your own different way."

Everything that came out of her mouth shocked me. Surely she was kidding.

"Pretty?" I asked, astounded.

"Yes. God!" she rolled her eyes. "You and that long, curly, dark hair. Even when it's a mess, it looks great. You rock those little glasses you wear during class and your eyes are, like, electric blue. How could you think you're anything but pretty? And god! Why am I having to explain this to you, anyway? You're smart enough to see it for yourself!"

I sat there at my desk, stunned and speechless. The girl I had just called a slut thought I was pretty? How could that be? Weren't pretty people always popular? Because popular was something I definitely wasn't. Not in high school, and not here. And, wait a minute, why was the girl I had hated for years telling me all of this? Was this part of some weird plan she had created to somehow embarrass me? I wasn't sure whether to be cautious or appreciative of her uncharacteristic compliments.

I mean, come on, the only experience I had with boys was being in a variety of clubs back in high school, and that lone boy I dated my senior year. I wasn't sure Nathan even counted as an official boyfriend, more as a friend who also happened to be a boy. Nathan was the valedictorian of our senior class and I was the salutatorian, so it was expected that we at least go out. I'm not sure why, but that was the way things had always been done at Northbrook, and I wasn't about to remake history. We rarely had the same classes and hardly saw each other at school. The couple of times we met for dinner, we were always rushing to get home to finish our schoolwork.

However, I went through a short phase in which I was determined to be as romantic and appealing as my brother. I practiced my flirting in the bathroom mirror and tested different types of smiles. I actually got Nathan to kiss me once, but I was pretty sure it was only so I would stop acting so weird. He never said anything, but I bet he hated it.

Wrenching my thoughts back to the present, I focused my attention once again on Brooke. She had relaxed her aggressive stance a little, but her eyes were still narrowed and piercing.

"What is it?" she demanded.

"Um, well, I didn't think you even knew who I was," I said slowly, not wanting to spark her to anger again.

"I live here too, you know," she responded.

"I meant in high school. I only knew you from a distance, and I didn't think you even knew I existed."

"Well, I did and I do," she said. I thought I detected a hint of nervousness in her comment, but it was gone before I could be sure.

"Okay…" I conceded.

"Here," she said, picking up my cell phone and tossing it back to me. "You can go back to talking to whoever that was." She swept out of the room regally, closing the door firmly behind her. I stared at the place where she had stood and realized I was shaking with amazement and fear.

*   *   *

Weeks passed and I was still puzzled about my confrontation with Brooke. I had no logical reason to believe that anything she'd said was the truth. I tried to analyze and sort out some of the puzzle pieces with Dan, explaining what had happened with Brooke, but not daring to give away too much. However, Dan and Brooke had had a minor fling in high school, so while he was sympathetic to my problems, he was much more interested in hearing about her. Their relationship, like many of hers, had lasted less than a week, but I knew he still had feelings for her. All the boys in high school did.

One day, during a break between classes, I stopped in the Quad and looked around. Fall was in full bloom and the change in weather was noticeable not only by the larger coats and hats, but by the way everyone's heads ducked against the wind when they exited buildings. October brought with it a biting, cold wind that found its way inside every coat and jacket. The sun was out, but there had already been a brief spit of snow earlier in the week; everyone knew winter was on its way.

There were not many people in the Quad, on account of the weather. Obviously people developed different places to congregate when the temperature dropped, but I had grown accustomed to the crowds so the Quad appeared strangely empty. As I gazed at the collection of people who were out braving the elements, my eyes zeroed in on the strange girl from my English class and the boy from the library couch. They were seated together on a bench with an older blonde guy between them. He didn't look like the typical college student, but I guessed that he was probably a graduate student advising his undergraduate friends...or something like that.

Clustered around the bench were about 10 other kids, and all of them were vaguely similar. All were relatively thin, and very physically fit. In our previous interactions, I hadn't really noticed the book girl's shape, but from where I was standing it was obvious she was muscular, in a well-toned, physically fit kind of way. I had always been skinny, with less muscle tone than a baby deer. Dan often joked that I had 'deer legs,' all skinny and wobbly. I felt a little self-conscious before I steeled myself against the comparison. All of the kids in the cluster wore dark colors like black, gray, and navy, and that made them stand out from the brightly lit buildings. I was sure they intended the opposite effect.

I watched as a girl in a bright blue NorthFace bounced over and positioned herself in front of a girl with very blonde hair, who sat on the ground at the feet of the 'book girl.' The bouncy girl pointed to a book she held and gestured wildly, no doubt asking something about the latest homework assignment.

The rest of the group quietly observed the interaction, but none of them spoke during the two girls' conversation. After a few minutes, they finished talking, and the bouncy girl waved, and trotted back to her original group. Ironically, her group was also dressed alike, but in brightly colored jackets and wool caps. I guessed that they must be cheer-leaders, due to the overly bright colors and their constant and annoying perkiness.

I was still a few paces away from the group, but class would start soon and I knew I had to move faster. My pathway through the Quad took me closer to them with every step. I tried to remain calm and disinterested, but this serious group of students dominated my full attention. None of them looked at me as I passed by, save one. The older one, the grad student, glanced up as I passed, studying me intently before returning his attention to the others.

Economics, my least favorite subject, was as boring as usual. Professor Kwon spoke poor English. His grasp of the language wasn't completely off the charts awful, but it was bad enough that you had to really concentrate to understand him. I always brought a pocket recorder with me so I could replay the lecture and catch things I may have missed the first time around. In reality, I'm not sure recording the lecture really helped in this case, because I loathed the subject matter. Shocking, I know, that a smart girl wouldn't like the math and equations that come with economics, but it's the cold, hard truth.

On my way back to Drayhorn, I looked to see if the peculiar group was still there, but they were gone. The entire Quad was empty.

Dan

"All right men! Let's move!"

Bodies flew toward each other at record speed. The team had been running this same play all day, but we weren't going to get a rest until we got it right. October, the height of our season, and Coach was treating us like it was the first week of practice. The evening air was crisp and I could see my own breath in front of my face as I waited for his next instructions.

"That was pitiful! That is not going to help us beat Alabama next Saturday!" Coach bellowed. "Do it again!"

We were losing energy and momentum with every run-through. Two of the assistant coaches pleaded with Coach to stop running the same play and get on with other drills, but he wouldn't hear of it.

"*Run it again!*" he demanded.

We ran that same play over and over, again and again, until we finally got it right. When Coach at last gave a satisfied sigh, the whole team collapsed on the field with our chests heaving. We were totally exhausted.

"Good job, boys. We're done for today."

Liz

The first significant snowfall of the year came at the end of October. The semester was in full swing, and people scurried back and forth through the walls of white, spending as little time out in the freezing cold as possible. As I walked through the snow toward the library, I leaned my head back to catch some of the fast-falling flakes on my upturned face. Around me, white spheres whizzed back and forth as some students started an impromptu battle. Some of the snowballs nailed their intended targets while others missed by a mile.

"Hello, there," said a voice to my right. I turned, a little startled since I had been caught up watching the snowball fight. Walking beside me was the older-looking blonde guy I had seen with the book girl and the couch boy. I still hadn't caught any of their names.

"You are Liz, right?" he asked, smiling. I nodded, unsure of what to do or say, and wondering how he knew my name. I nervously focused my eyes on the ground, half-praying for him to vanish as quickly as he had appeared.

"I almost didn't recognize you in your hat," he said conversationally. My hand flew up to my hat out of habit, my fingers rearranging the white knit fabric that kept my curls at bay. As my fingers touched it, I realized that the fabric was soaked from the thick flurries that had descended on my head. I sneaked another glance sideways. There I was, freezing, so much so that my teeth were beginning to chatter, but he looked completely comfortable in the vast whiteness; he only wore a light jacket but he didn't appear to be cold. His platinum blonde hair practically shone as the melted flakes reflected the light from the lampposts. He looked almost beautiful. A street lamp illuminated a glimmer of gold jewelry that peeked out beneath his light jacket. While staring at him, I became aware that I had stopped breathing, and inhaled quickly in an embarrassing gulp.

"Oh, yeah, um, hi," I said, as I felt my cheeks flush red. "Yeah, I'm Liz."

He laughed. "Well, hi yourself. I am Lio." He stuck out a gloved hand. I dragged mine from the comfort of my coat pocket and shook his.

"So…what are you reading?" he said, eyeing the book that was clutched to my chest by my other hand.

"Fantasy…romance…adventure…" I said noncommittally, hugging the book closer so he couldn't see the title.

"Sounds interesting. Does the book have a title?" he asked.

"Nope."

"No title?"

"Yep, no title."

"Then it does not qualify as a book," he said matter-of-factly.

"Fine. I'll tell you the title of this book if you tell me the title of the book your friend was reading," I replied.

"Which friend?"

"The girl with the dark hair in my English class, the one I keep seeing you with."

"Anna?" he suggested.

"Yeah, Anna."

"That might be hard. Anna reads a lot of books." He tilted his head to the side; his eyebrows knitted in concentration.

"Well, this one had brown leather binding and gold on the inside cover and—"

"Oh! My goodness! I just realized I am going to be late! It was lovely talking to you! Bye Liz!" he called over his shoulder, already trotting in the opposite direction, back the way we'd come. He was moving a bit too quickly for the standard walk.

Why is everyone trying to escape from me lately? I wondered. "Bye," I said softly, to no one in particular.

*　　*　　*

The random comings and goings of the mysterious group of people, and specifically my interaction with Lio, had sparked my interest. I went to the library to read every day that week, specifically blocking out chunks of time in my daily schedule, just to see if any of them would be on the couch when I got there. The student in me couldn't resist a good experiment, so I switched up the times every day, hoping to catch someone when they least expected me. But, again and again I was disappointed, and ended up alone on my little corner couch.

By the time Saturday morning came, I had pretty much given up. If these mysterious people were purposely avoiding me, then fine. But they could forget about getting their couch back. I half-ran to the library that afternoon after completing my homework, intent on claiming my favorite spot. As usual, the two-seater was empty when I arrived. I curled up on the right side of the couch, and panned the room, glaring at the empty bookcases surrounding me, silently daring anyone hiding behind them to come forth.

Within minutes, a giant snowball crashed into the tiny window on the far right wall. The deafening boom snapped me out of my "reading coma" and made me look up in alarm. Once I realized what had happened, I turned back to my book, and almost screamed out loud. There she was, the same mysterious girl, sitting on the other end of the couch not a foot away. I gaped at her. I hadn't heard her come in, and hadn't even felt her sit down. But there she was. She glanced at the book I held up against my mouth to stifle my scream. My eyes were wide with the shock of both the snowball's crash and her instant appearance. She rolled her half-lidded eyes and uttered a disgusted grunt.

"Interview with a Vampire...*fascinating*," she said, the last word dripping with sarcasm.

"You're Anna, right?" I managed to ask casually. Her head snapped up so fast it was a blur and her eyes were wide in alarm. It was obvious I had taken her off guard by knowing her name.

"How did you....?"

"I talked to some guy named Lio the other day," I said

with a small measure of pride. "I asked about you, and he told me your name." I shrugged, as if it was not important, but her reaction told me differently. Her eyes narrowed as she stared at me with a mix of wonder and panic.

"You…talked to Lio?" she stammered, her body poised to run if that was called for. "But he never talks to…"

"Never talks to whom?" I inquired, trying to maintain as casual a tone as possible, but desperately hoping she would give me more information about her mysterious friends before she darted away.

"Hu—" she faltered. "I mean, few, few people. He talks to very few people…" She appeared to be torn between running away from me and sticking around to see what else I knew. No matter how easy-going she tried to sound, I could see worry and doubt in her eyes. Cornered, she tried to turn the attention back to me.

"What did you say your name was again?"

"I never got a chance to say, but my name is Liz," I replied, struggling to keep my voice even. "Nice to actually meet you. What are you reading?"

The gold book she clutched in her hands was upside down, the face, and thus the title, turned toward her lap. Like a four-year-old child caught with her hand in the cookie jar, she pushed the book behind her on the couch.

"What book?" she said innocently.

Now this was a surprise. *Who does she think she is fooling?* I thought. I never was one for childish acts, so I said, "Really? Are we really going to pretend you didn't have a book in your hands just now?"

"I don't know what you're talking about," Anna said as she brought her hands around to the front. "What book?" She stood up and motioned toward the couch to emphasize her words. When I looked at the place she'd been sitting, the brown book was gone.

I mean, gone. Vanished, moved, disappeared, not there. I leaned over and reached behind the cushions to make sure there were no traces of a book, as my confused brain tried to piece together this strange sequence of events.

"But...you just had it...How did you...Where did you put it?"

Anna turned around, her hands held high in the air, as if to emphasize her innocence. Her clothes were snug and dark. It was clear she hadn't hidden the book in them.

"What is *with* you?" I asked.

She looked puzzled. "What do you mean?"

"I tried to ask you about the book the other day and you totally ignored me. Then, I tried to ask that Lio guy about you and about the book, and he practically ran away from me. Now you—"

"You talked to Lio about the book?" she asked, interrupting my rant. Her voice went down to no more than a whisper, followed by a charged silence that seemed to fill the area. "I've got to go," she said suddenly, and darted back through the rows of bookshelves toward the main part of the library.

"Anna, wait!" I called out, but she was already too far away to hear me.

Liz

It was days before I saw Anna or Lio again. It was like they had disappeared. On the bright side, I had the reading couch all to myself, and I used the opportunity to zoom through book after book.

A few days before Thanksgiving break, I started my daily trip to the library. The nearly continuous snowfall had accumulated into drifts so high they were stacked up over my head. Every once in awhile, I could see tunnels, evidence that kids with too much time on their hands had carved forts into the frozen white walls. No doubt some of their snowball fights had escalated into hardcore wars that necessitated sturdy forts.

I had once again brought my favorite Anne Rice novel to pass the time. Although I had read it numerous times already, I felt connected to the fantasy life of the mythical creatures she created and described. I had just settled into the couch with my book in front of my face, when I heard a slight but distinctive cough. I looked up slowly, half expecting to see Anna, and was surprised to see Lio's shock of blonde hair and dark blue eyes.

"Hi," he said, grinning at my startled expression.

"Hey," I breathed, once I managed to recover.

"Sorry about having to leave so suddenly last time we

talked. There was something really important I needed to see about. I hope you do not think me rude," he said with a flirty grin.

I nodded awkwardly, unable to speak, completely mesmerized. He looked like a dream; exactly like a character right out of my book. Not in a romantic way, more in an ethereal way. Somehow, Lio's physical appearance was like a combination of all the leading men in my favorite novels. He wasn't perfect or overly handsome, just unreal, like he wasn't a part of this world. I hadn't noticed before but he spoke very formally, with a slight Spanish accent. I found myself gazing deeply into his deep blue eyes, totally captivated. It felt like there was so much to learn about him, a vast expanse of knowledge buried there in his eyes.

"What is it?" he asked, scrutinizing my face as he tried to figure out why I was staring. I blinked rapidly to pull myself out of the trance I had unintentionally fallen into, and my thoughts returned to reality.

"Nothing," I laughed nervously.

"Interview with a Vampire?" he asked, eyeing my reading material.

"Yeah," I said breathlessly, relieved to talk about something I was comfortable with. "It's a personal favorite."

"It is your favorite? Really? Why?"

"I don't know, I guess because it's easy to get lost in their world. I feel more at home reading this kind of book than anything else…"

"Fantasy, huh?"

"M-hmm…"

Our conversation had officially reached an awkward silence. I was nervous and fidgety, and he looked the same, though I couldn't imagine why. I tried not to stare at him and his eyes darted around the room as if searching for something to talk about. I also scanned the room, looking for anything to focus on but his face. But for some reason, I couldn't stop myself. I kept returning my gaze to his beautiful face. Not only was I staring, my heart was beating a million miles an hour, so loudly that I was surprised I was the only one who seemed to hear it.

"So here's a question," I said abruptly, daring myself to step outside of my comfort zone. He raised his eyebrows playfully, yet apprehensively.

"What's the deal with the wall over there?" I pointed to the wall across from the couch and Lio looked a little confused.

"I do not know what you mean…"

"The first time I was here, there was a guy sitting here as well, and I only got through a couple words of my book before he vanished without a trace. The next time, Anna was on the couch and she basically refused to talk to me. When I finally got her to say something, I asked where the first guy had gone and she told me he was through that wall," I pointed. "Then she disappeared just like the first guy. But there's nothing there! It's two feet of wall and brick and then outside, so what's up with that?"

Lio's eyes narrowed as his gaze drifted to the empty white space. He shifted uncomfortably, and I caught a quick glimpse of a medallion hanging around his neck, but as he moved, it slipped back under his clothes before

I got a good look.

"That wall is not something you need to worry about."

"But, what about—"

"I mean it. You do not need to worry that pretty little head of yours over something that does not concern you. Now, I have to find Alita…" Suddenly Lio was off the couch and walking toward the front of the library in his typical brisk fashion, smoothly and skillfully dodging bookshelves and people, even at that speed.

"Okay…" I said, even though I couldn't imagine why the wall would be that big of a deal. He couldn't possibly believe I would forget about what he said. This was the second time he had bolted away from a conversation with me after I asked something difficult, or maybe uncomfortable. I was mystified at what might be going through his head or what he was trying to prove. Plus, he had said he needed to find Alita. Who was she?

Seven

Lianco

I half-ran from the small couch in the corner of the library. I was seething with fury and was barely able to disguise it from the humans in the library who watched my hasty exit with wide eyes. Poor Liz had done nothing wrong, but I was pretty sure she felt differently. Unfortunately, she was only a helpless pawn in the middle of a complex plan.

ALITA! I forcefully projected my thoughts to her all the way across campus, unable to control the rage that bubbled inside me.

Yes? Her voice in my head was as pure and clear as if we were speaking to face to face, just like always.

My office. NOW!

Okay, okay, just give me a minute.... came the reply.

No delays. I said now and I mean it!

I heard you! Geez...

I burst through the alternate entrance to the Realm, not even bothering to make sure I was not followed or seen. I heard the three guards groan, and I almost smiled with satisfaction, but immediately thought better of it. My hurried entrance through the outer Film had caused part of protective membrane that served as a doorway to shatter. This meant that someone from the Seiku Council, the highest ranking wizards in the Seiku sector, would be sent to fix it.

The Seikus tried to impose their way of doing things on everyone and everything, with no exceptions. That was their nature. No doubt the three guards, who possessed such an incredibly low understanding of the inner workings of the Alliance, much less of Seiku magic, would be forced to suffer through a long, tedious lecture on the importance of effective security while the Film was fixed.

Alita was already waiting for me in my office, her fingers drumming impatiently on the mahogany desktop.

"Right on time," I said, greeting her with a slight nod of my head. "Impressive…and somewhat unusual."

"Well, you know how I hate going slow," she grinned mischievously, her teeth glinting in the low lighting.

"I heard you broke the Film," she said teasingly, eyebrows raised, waiting for my rebuttal.

"How in the world do you get information so quickly?" I replied, my eyes betraying my frustration behind an otherwise perfect mask. She pointed toward the ceiling, at the tiny, winged creatures darting back and forth, and smiled.

"You have to get with the times, old man," Alita mocked affectionately. "Imps are officially *the* fastest way to send and receive information."

I raised my own eyebrows in return, knowing I still had the upper hand. *Really?* I directed my thoughts at her. *Faster than allreçu?*

"Well, not counting *allreçu*," she said aloud. You and I are the only ones who can project our thoughts…" Her eyes fell as she trailed off, and I knew what was coming next. "Well, besides him…"

"Besides Serenu, you mean?" I tried to sound sympa-thetic but the words came out in a bitter tone.

"He's not all bad!" she protested. I could tell she was still hurting, and somewhat embarrassed by her association with him.

"Maybe not in the past, but you and I both know how things stand now. You know as well as I do what he did and what he is capable of."

"You don't know anything…"

I took a deep breath and switched the subject back to my original topic. "Well, since you seem to get all the news before anyone else, you know why I called you here, right?"

"Maybe," she smiled. Her shoulders relaxed and I could tell that the uncomfortable tension had evaporated. As a Seiku, she was never one to pass up gloating over having information, even if it was about her.

"Alita, you know the code; you overstepped your bound-aries. Even if Liz is one of us, or if they both are, they need to figure it out on their own."

"But if the war is coming, we need to be ready!" she argued. "We don't have time to wait! We need her! We need *them!*"

"I know," I said softly, my voice barely a whisper. The thoughts in my head were racing around so fast I could not keep track of them. "If they do not figure it out soon, we could all be doomed. But the code stands."

Alita looked frustrated, torn between what she knew was right and what her impulsive nature tempted her to do.

"Sir!" came a deep voice from the doorway.

I looked over Alita's shoulder. I did not appreciate the interruption and uncharacteristically let it show on my face.

"Yes?" I asked frostily.

"Um, w-well, s-sir," Logos, the gigantic chief guard, stammered. My cold stare obviously affected the clarity of his feeble-minded thoughts. "Um, y-you see…"

"Oh, get on with it!" Alita snapped. She had no problem being curt or even rude; her impatience often took over and got the better of her.

"Yes ma'am!" Logos grinned from ear to ear. Rudeness from Alita was characteristic, and the familiarity gave him focus. "We have a bit of a problem…"

Liz

I felt chilly and alone as I walked back to my dorm. I pulled my coat closer, and tightened the scarf around my neck, but I could feel the cold seeping in more and more. As I walked, I got the eerie feeling someone was watching me. Maybe it was just the darkness or my mind playing tricks, but I felt a thousand eyes on me, watching, waiting.

Just then a man stepped out from behind Drayhorn, not fifteen yards from me. His features were so dark they almost blended with the night. His skin was very tan, and his long, shaggy hair blew around his face in the crisp night air. My feet slowed to a stop and I hardly dared to breathe. The air felt thick with anticipation and something else— something sinister.

The man was tall, thin, and muscular looking. Despite his dark features, his teeth gleamed white in the black of night as he opened his mouth to speak.

"You're Liz, right?" He spoke so softly that I thought perhaps I hadn't heard him out loud as much as heard him in my head. When he walked toward me, I noticed that his footsteps made no imprints on the grass. Fear stopped my breathing altogether.

"I've heard so much about you," he continued, his slow pace never faltering.

Despite my brain's best efforts to tell me to run, my feet were frozen in place. I heard a faint rustling behind me and, at the same time, noticed the man suddenly stopped his approach and grinned.

"Hello, brother," he said icily.

I became acutely aware of three other people around me. Lio appeared and stood to my right.

"Serenu," Lio replied, in a quiet voice completely void of emotion.

"Well isn't this a happy little reunion," Serenu mocked. "Mother would have been so proud."

"You are not supposed to be out," Lio said conversationally, "even though I know how much you love to play in the dark."

I looked around, helpless and considerably confused. *Brothers?* The two couldn't be any more different. My brain whirled as I tried to figure out what was happening. Two other men standing behind me stepped slightly forward, but I didn't recognize either of them in the darkness.

"Well, as much as I *love* reunions, looks like I really should be on my way," Serenu smirked, turning his back on us. Our group watched as he sauntered away. A good three or four seconds went by before Lio exhaled audibly.

"Go."

The two men behind me sprang to life and raced after the figure, now barely visible in the night. I gasped, nervous about what might happen when they caught him. Just before the two men reached their target, however, he vanished into the night. My jaw dropped, my head spun, and everything went black.

Nine

Lianco

I watched with disgust as my brother disappeared into the night. He called for the portal to the Unknown and disappeared between the Realms. Serenu was not even truly my brother, only a half-brother. We were born of the same mother; Serenu first, and then me a few years later.

Serenu's father was Loki, a man rightly named after the god of evil, blackness, and trickery. Loki was one of the most powerful Beings this side of the Unknown, famous for his creativity with magic. Loki had been the first child born from a multi-sector union; his parents were from Seiku and Leku, and he inherited his father's Seiku powers. As a young man, Loki was well-known and well-liked, and when my mother, a Roku, met him, she instantly fell in love. Not long after, they conceived a baby, Serenu, and he was born a Roku like our mother. Loki was disappointed. Loki wanted his son to be dually talented, since no child in the Alliance had ever been born with two powers. However, Serenu did not fulfill his father's dreams.

It was not until Serenu was five or six years old that Loki revealed his true nature. The jealousy, anger, and evil inside him inherently rose up and began to ruin him. The once protective father became a menace and a danger to his own family. The worst of it was that Serenu seemed to derive pleasure from his father's increasing cruelty, no matter how disturbingly wicked he was.

My mother, Nephy, walked out on Loki after one of his many tirades left her completely singed down her right side. In fact, it was in the healing room of the Leku that my mother and father first met.

Larenon was one of the most powerful healers the Alliance had even seen; equally as powerful as Loki, but in a more positive area. After my father healed my mother, she begged him to do something about the child she had brought with her who was still wailing for his father. Serenu was placed under the care of Olli, one of the older healers who had a fondness for children. My mother was instantly drawn to Larenon's calm, sincere, compassionate nature, perhaps because it was the opposite of her first husband's.

I was born sometime later, and ironically inherited the dual powers that my half brother's father craved. I was the only dual Being born since the beginning of the Alliance. I inherited my father's Leku abilities, but neither of my parents ever figured out where my Seiku ability had come from. Not only was I the first dual Being, but one of my powers had not come from either parent. It was a mystery that no one had ever solved.

Both my parents carefully tended to my upbringing, nurturing me with love and teaching me the skills necessary to master both of my powers and more. I learned the healing ways of the Leku from my father and sat through my lessons in the Seiku sector with no complaints. I was also taught to fight in the ways of the Roku by my mother, who felt I might need added protection one day.

The unhappiest days of my childhood were those when I was forced to visit my half brother in his home with Olli. Once a week, Serenu and I spent our 'bonding time' glaring at each other for hours until my mother arrived to take me home. Although she saw him each time, my mother refused to acknowledge Serenu, never paying attention to him, even when he was in the same room. I could not understand why I was forced to spend any time with this half-brother if she did not even acknowledge his presence, but whenever I asked my mother about it, my questions went unanswered.

Serenu was obviously jealous of me, though he would never admit it. I had everything he wanted: dual abilities, parents, and affection. His own father, Loki, had disappeared shortly after my mother left him, and had not been seen for years. No one knew exactly where he had gone, but many speculated he had retreated to the Unknown. Many Beings gossiped about the scandal, and Serenu often felt the sting of the rumors whispered behind his back. His anger grew and much of it was directed at me. At last, I became old enough to refuse to see him, no matter how much my mother tried to goad me into it. It did not matter, though. After a while, Serenu was old enough for his qualifying test.

Beings of the Alliance grow at a human rate until age eighteen. After that, our aging process slows significantly, so many of us live to be five or six hundred years old. So, when my half-brother turned eighteen, he was fully prepared for his qualifying test, which determines if a student is prepared to become a full member of the Alliance, or if they require additional training. If a student requires extra training such that they must take the test twice, they are basically considered second class citizens in their specific sector. On the day of his test, my mother visited Serenu—the first time she had done so since placing him in Olli's care. It is possible that my mother's visit affected him strongly, but whatever the reason, Serenu did not test well. The Seiku Council that oversaw his test determined that he would require extra training. Their verdict ruined Serenu's chances of becoming a successful Seiku like his father, and sent him into a fit of rage, one of the most vicious episodes I ever saw.

Many Alliance members were injured and one was almost killed as a result of his anger; however, before anyone could apprehend him, he disappeared into the depths of the Unknown, an ability he had no doubt inherited from his father. No one could follow him, and no one wanted to.

Serenu eventually returned to the human realm. When he did, he was captured and exiled to the Abyss. The Abyss was the Alliance's prison, a bottomless pit that promised death from all sides. The sides of the pit had tiny ledges that prisoners fought to stay on. No one who had fallen into the depths of the Abyss had ever survived, and not even the highest-ranking Alliance members knew where it led. Serenu rotted away in the Abyss for more than ten decades, out surviving other prisoners with trickery and deceit. He became the sort of 'ghost story' figure mothers scare their children with. At the time, we didn't know that he had surreptitiously spent those 100 years building up his power, using the other prisoners as test subjects for his spells. Eventually, he used his power to break out of the Abyss, a feat no one else had ever accomplished. Serenu escaped to the Unknown once again, no doubt planning his revenge.

I wrenched my mind back to the present, to the crumpled form of a girl in front of me. Serenu had fled into his beloved Unknown, again, and one of the Legends lay unconscious near my feet. Darien and Orion trotted back toward me, obviously frustrated they had not captured Serenu in time. Orion picked Liz up effortlessly.

"I saw this girl in the library back in August," Darien chuckled. "She was sitting next to Olli's grandson…what's his name?"

Orion began to struggle, however, and Liz nearly fell out of his arms. "Damn, she's not as light as she looks," Orion exclaimed as he shifted his weight in order to provide for hers. "Help me out here, Darien."

"Nah, man," Darien grinned, "I think you have it."

"Come *on*," Orion wheezed

"Take her to the Leku," I said quietly. "I will see to her there."

They set off, Orion still staggering a little under the dead weight of Liz's body on his shoulder.

Careful! I sent at them.

Darien raised one hand in reply. I turned back to the sidewalk and stared into the darkness. Though the fog was rapidly thickening, I could see another figure slowly coming toward me. I knew her loping gait well, even in the darkness.

"Alita."

"That was him, wasn't it?" she asked quietly.

"Yes," I ran my hand through my hair in frustration.

"How could he…where did he…?

"Who knows?" I spat. "And frankly, who cares?" I was past being angry. I was furious with myself for being so stupid and for letting the monster get away. Alita cringed and half turned away.

I care, came her reply in my head, so soft and meek I almost was not sure I had heard it.

I know, I responded with a big exhale.

"What's going to happen to Liz?" she inquired cautiously, not wanting to test me if I was still angry.

"I do not know." Again, my hand wound its way through my hair. "I sent Liz with Darien and Orion to the Leku sterile rooms. She is currently unconscious, so we will have to see what she remembers once she wakes up."

"I still think you should break the news to her sooner or later. And by that I mean sooner, not later." She smirked, obviously pleased with her clever sarcasm.

Do I need to remind you of the code?

Stop being an old fart! Who gives a crap about the code?

Liz

I had never been unconscious in my life. It was a weird feeling, something like drowning, except not in water but in a pool of blackness with no way to swim to the top. I felt pressure from all sides, almost like the air was solid. It was not a pleasant experience.

Even in my unconscious state, I could hear voices calling my name, but I couldn't tell who they were or what direction they were coming from. The voices got louder and seemed closer, but when I looked around in the darkness for any sign of who might be speaking, there was no one. I tried to cry out but I worried that the heavy blackness surrounding me would fill my lungs if I so much as dared to open my mouth. Frantically, I searched for a way out of the miserable black. In the distance, one single speck of light broke a hole in the darkness. The thin beam grew, and I swam toward the hole. It got closer and closer until I was able to push myself through and—

My eyelids fluttered open. Unfocused and a bit dazed, my eyes slowly swept the room, taking in the blurred shapes that I guessed were people.

"She's waking up," I heard someone say.

"Good, then it is working," said another voice.

"Wha—," I tried to talk, but my mouth felt glued

together, thick and unusable.

"Just relax, everything is going to be fine," the first voice said soothingly. "Lie still and give yourself a chance to recover."

Although I was usually an obedient person, my mind screamed in protest. I tried to sit up, but large, strong hands held me back.

"Sir!" said the owner of the hands, "the girl is waking up!" The booming voice was gruff and uncertain, and the form that hid the light from my eyes was gigantic.

"Uh—," I started again, but the effort of the words was too much. My tongue felt heavy and too big for my mouth.

"We know she's waking up, you *egghead!*" My head was clear enough that I distinctly recognized the second voice as feminine.

"Be nice," the male voice replied in a calm, even tone. My eyes were still unfocused. I wanted desperately to make out the blurred blends of yellow, black, and white. "Just keep her still, Logos. I need the healing to set in."

So Logos was the owner of the large hands that held me down with enormous strength. At the mention of healing, I held very still, obeying the kind, male voice. I sensed he could help me. I blinked again and again in an attempt to see through the blur, and then suddenly, everything in the room became clear. All the objects and people were crystal clear. Involuntarily, my hands flew to my face, searching for my glasses. I gasped at their absence, amazed by my much improved vision.

"Feeling better?" A shock of blonde hair crossed into

view and I smiled at Lio. I opened my mouth slightly in preparation for a greeting, but he quickly snapped my jaw shut.

"Do not try to talk just yet, your mouth still will not work." He smiled. "Now, tell me, or rather, show me, are you hurt anywhere? I need to know if the healing is spreading over your entire body."

My eyebrows shot up in a quizzical look. *Healing?* I thought. *What healing? Is he messing with me?*

"What he means is medicine. Is the medicine is working? Do you have any pain?" Blonde hair turned to black as library girl Anna's face loomed before me. Anna turned away slightly, and whatever look she shot Lio obviously embarrassed him.

"Right. Medicine," Lio said sheepishly. "So, does it hurt anywhere? Just shake your head yes or no."

I shook my head no because I had no physical pain. The only pain was the frustration of wanting to communicate and being unable to do so. My mouth was still against me. I watched as Lio looked abruptly to his left at Anna, who stared pointedly back at him. His eyebrows knitted together with concern or irritation, and she bugged her eyes out glaring back in his direction. Their silent exchange of looks lasted no more than a minute; it was almost as if they were having an argument I couldn't hear. My eyes darted back and forth in an attempt to follow the imaginary conversation, but it was a futile exercise—like watching a ping pong match with no ball.

My neck started to hurt from swiveling left and right,

and then Lio gave a resigned sigh. He ran a hand through his hair and turned to face me. In a flash, his other hand flew straight at my face and stopped millimeters from the tip of my nose. He snapped his fingers, and I thought I heard him mutter something under his breath.

All of the disgusting gunk in my mouth disappeared instantly. I rolled my tongue around a few times, then slowly opened my mouth, pretty sure that I could now speak.

"How…" I started, testing my own abilities, "how did you do that?" I glanced toward Anna, whose back was now toward me, and at Lio whose face was inches from mine.

"How…"

He put one finger to my lips.

"What if I…what if *we* told you that you were special?"

Eleven

Lianco

I watched Liz's face transition from looking curious, to confused, and then to dumbfounded.

I knew this was not the right thing! I shot nervously at Alita. *I told you!*

She frowned. *We just have to explain it to her! She's a smart girl, she'll be fine with it. God, get a hold of yourself!*

I sighed, and turned back to Liz, searching for the right words to explain the situation without upsetting her even more.

"What I mean is, we believe that you are a very special person...someone we have been waiting for a very long time." Liz raised her eyebrows at my words.

Go to Neku and see if they have been able to dig up any more information on Liz, I sent at Alita.

Why can't I stay here?

Very well, get Darien to do it. I need you to go get Dan anyway.

What?!

Just go get him and bring him here.

She glared at me, then slid silently over to the door, which opened to reveal a clearly shocked and ashamed eavesdropping Darien. I caught his eye just before Alita slipped out of the room and gave him a hard, scolding glare. It did not occur to me that Liz and I were alone until she cleared her throat. I turned to face her and was grateful to find an expectant expression on her face rather than an anxious one, as if she already knew what I was going to say.

"So…" she began, "what's this about my being special?"

I was only half-listening to her words. The other half of my attention was focused on any thoughts coming in from Alita. The curious thing was that I was picking up two trains of thought. One was silent, which I knew to be Alita's, and the other was also silent, but mixed with static. There was an extra murmur on the second thought line, a steady stream of sounds that were not words yet sounded coherent.

"Lio?"

I half-jumped where I stood. My attention had strayed solely to my thoughts, and Liz's voice brought me back quickly.

"Yes? Sorry." I cursed myself inwardly for not paying full attention to her. My hand followed its all too familiar pathway through my hair.

"What is going on?" Liz demanded, her eyes now surprisingly fierce and questioning.

"It is more complicated than you can understand," I replied.

"Too complicated for me? Well that's a new one," she laughed harshly. "How dumb do you think I am?"

"No, it is not a matter of intelligence, really—"

"Then what is it a matter of and how do you know I won't understand it?" She propped herself up on her elbows on the sterile table.

"Well—"

"I mean, really! Who made you the judge of how smart I am?" She was angry now. She stood up, crossed her arms, and began pacing the room.

"It is just that—"

"It's just what? It's just that you don't think I have any sense? Who are you to tell me that—"

"Liz!" I practically shouted. She turned abruptly from her pacing to stare at me. "We need your brother Dan to be here before we can explain everything," I said. "We need you two together."

"What do you mean you need my brother here? What does he have to do with it? And who is 'we' anyway? At least tell me where I am."

"Liz, please calm down. I will tell you everything once Dan arrives. Alita should be back with him very soon. "

Liz sighed, exasperated, and started pacing again. I watched her brown curls fly around her face as she whipped around at each end of the room. She had made about three trips back and forth when she suddenly stopped. Her expression turned to one of confusion and defense.

"How is Dan going to be here soon when he's hours away? How do you even know about him anyway?"

Liz

Confusion. A little panic. Anger. That's what my mind was experiencing. It was pretty evident that I had been kidnapped and was now being held against my will, but something deep inside told me I was there for a reason.

All the different pieces of information were spinning around inside my head. How was Dan going to arrive soon when I knew he was hours away at UT? I had never mentioned my brother to any of them, so how did they even know about Dan? I didn't realize I had said the words out loud until I saw Lio's expression change.

"Um…uh…well…" he stammered. I raised one eyebrow. "You told me about Dan that day in the library."

"We hardly talked that day in the library! How do you know about him?" I demanded shrilly. As president and lead prosecutor of the mock trial club in high school, interrogation was my specialty. However, I knew I probably wasn't handling the questioning as professionally as I usually would, on account of my circumstances. Lio's faced paled even more at my question; so much, in fact, that it became difficult to distinguish where his face ended and his hair began. I almost smiled at how flustered he was, but I kept my face composed because I wanted answers.

"Alita will return very soon and you can ask her." He

turned his head toward the door, with his chin tilted slightly to the side in what I suppose he hoped looked like deep concentration.

"Alita?" I asked quietly.

I can't begin to describe how slowly he turned his head back to face me, and how much controlled anger was in his expression as he did. His eyes were narrowed, his hands clenched in fists. Involuntarily, I stepped back, alarmed by the sudden change in him.

"What?" His single word was hard and cold, stabbing into my ears like a knife blade.

"You said Alita will be right back," I said firmly, squaring my shoulders in an attempt to present a brave front. My resolve was broken, however, as he moved towards me, his face now calm and his hands relaxed.

"What nonsense are you coming up with now?" he said with a smile. An eerie shiver ran through me at the Dr. Jekyll and Mr. Hyde change in him.

"But you said—"

"Ssh." He put one finger to my lips. My feet tried to move backward but I was already against the wall. I looked around in a panic, trying to figure out how I had gotten against the wall and searching for a way out. There were no windows in the room, and no vents in the ceiling. The only way out was the door, and Lio was standing between it and me.

"Now," he said, putting his hands against the wall on either side of my head and lowering his face until his nose was literally inches from mine. I could see his eyes so clearly, as blue and as endless as the ocean. Once again, I felt myself drifting into them.

"Anna is coming back soon so you can redirect all of your questions to her."

He stepped back and turned away from me. I just stood there in shock, my back pressed against the wall, as tiny beads of sweat started to emerge on my forehead. I opened my mouth to speak but the door was flung open before I could utter a single syllable. Anna stood in the doorway, breathless and beaming.

"Guess who I found?!" she announced, stepping into the room and tugging on another hand, which was connected to a body hidden by the rest of the doorframe. The unseen person resisted, but Anna tugged hard and a boy with a hoodie on, head down, stumbled into the room.

"Ta-dah!" she cried happily, throwing back his hood. There, in all his glory, confusion written all over his face, stood my brother.

Thirteen

Dan

Dun! Dun! Dun! Dun! Dun! Dun! Dun! The monotonous sound of eighteen basketballs striking the floor, somewhat out of sync, was getting on my one last nerve. I was lazily dribbling around the court, watching my 17 other teammates, as we supposedly did our cool down for the day. I half-snorted to myself as I realized how ridiculous this team was. As punishment for a certain celebratory incident during a recent football game, Coach had assigned me to play on a recreational basketball team near campus. *This was supposed to teach me teamwork?* I thought ironically. The rec team was utterly dysfunctional; the guys played like 17 individuals instead of one team. So now, instead of just being a Volunteer on UT's football team, I was also a volunteer on the Mountain Park Eagles basketball team. Woo-freakin-hoo.

"Good practice boys! See you all on Saturday for the big game!" The ancient man who was the team's excuse for a coach could hardly croak out the words before he shuffled off the court.

I jogged to the bench. During practice I hadn't even broken a sweat, but the rest of the guys were dripping wet. This was not an in-shape group, and it clearly showed. I tossed a spare towel at one of the Eagles. He didn't catch it, so it landed on the floor. Typical.

"See you Saturday," I muttered, hurrying to my car. Zoe was waiting for me at the campus library, and I was already ten minutes late, thanks to this idiotic assignment. Señor Ancient needed to figure out a way to run practice a little faster next time—he was cutting into my social life. I threw the Mustang in high gear and whipped out of the gym's parking lot, narrowly missing the old coach as he hobbled to his rusty Oldsmobile.

When I pulled into to the library parking lot, I was only twenty minutes late, but Zoe wasn't waiting outside like we had agreed. Fortunately, I found a decent parking spot, a rare feat on campus, and pulled in. Stepping out of the car door was like stepping into the Arctic Circle. It was November and the nights were getting colder and colder in Knoxville. It didn't help that I still had my basketball shorts on because I had been in such a hurry. I threw on a hoodie and ran for the library door.

Damn, it's freezing out here, I thought, taking the steps up to the library two at a time. I looked around for a blotch of light against the dark gloom; Zoe's blonde head against a backdrop of dark buildings. I couldn't see a thing, the blackness was overwhelming. I heard the library door open behind me and turned to see a figure silhouetted by the light spilling out from inside the building.

"You're Dan, right?"

I stood dumbstruck, unable to see the face that belonged to a distinctly feminine voice.

"Yeah, and who are you?"

The figure moved away from the light, closer to me. My

eyes were adjusting a little and I could make out her shape, but not her features.

"I'm Alita."

"Hey…" the pause was long but not necessarily awkward. "I, uh, I gotta go inside," I said as I tried to move around her. She moved to block my path.

"Actually, you're needed elsewhere. Liz sent me to get you."

"Liz?" I mused. I wondered how this girl knew about my sister, since I had not mentioned her to many people at UT.

"Yes, Liz!" Alita said impatiently. "Now come on." She grabbed my hand and tugged me down the steps.

"I-I have a girlfriend!" I spluttered, taken aback at her aggression and a bit out of breath at her speed. This girl was strong and I was embarrassed at how easily she was dragging me away. The girlfriend remark was the only thing I could think of to slow her down.

"Spare me," came the sarcastic response. We hadn't run more than nine or ten seconds when we stopped short.

"Where are we?" I asked the girl I still couldn't see.

"The side of the library." Her girly, attractive voice was tainted with sarcasm. "Reach out and touch the wall."

The wall was a freezing cold barrier, each smooth brick outlined by the rough mortar around it. I heard muttering to my right, and turned to see Alita's silhouette once more, illuminated by a glowing sphere of light she held in her right hand. It was no bigger than a ping-pong ball, yet it gave off a bright light that spread all around us. The continuous rotation of blue swirls inside the ball was mesmerizing.

"How the hell…?" I whispered.

"Don't worry about it. There are a lot of things you don't understand yet. I need you to come with me," she implored. "*Liz* needs you to come with me."

I nodded, and against my better judgment, grabbed the hand she held out to me. She placed her other hand on the wall, pushing the glowing sphere into the bricks. The sphere disappeared for a moment, and then reappeared twice as bright on the wall in front of us. The light flowed like a river through the various channels of mortar, spreading out into a vertical rectangle. I stared, open-mouthed, as the door took shape, glowing on all sides.

"Ready?" she asked. I was so stunned I could only nod. Before I was really ready, she stepped forward, the glow washing over her as she disappeared within, dragging me behind her.

*   *   *

When I opened my eyes, the first thing I saw was a sea of white.

Shit, I thought, *I'm in heaven.*

As my eyes gradually focused, I realized I was looking at the ceiling of some building. That meant the hard surface I was lying on must be the floor.

"Awake yet?" I turned my head to see Alita, who was sitting against a wall not two feet from my left arm. Her knees were drawn up to her chest and she rested her chin on top of them.

"Hold out your hand," she said. I tentatively raised my palm to receive a pinch of some shiny powder she held out in her fingers. "Swallow it," she commanded.

I didn't dare disobey. This whole scenario was too weird, and I certainly wasn't in a position to argue with this powerful girl. As soon as the powder hit my stomach, my heavy limbs suddenly felt fine. She stood up and I followed, still a little shaky from all I had been through. I mean, who walks through a wall and lives to tell about it? Evidently that powder she gave me had a big dose of caffeine or something in it because energy surged through my body and my vision cleared instantly, though I noticed my tongue was a little swollen.

"Put your hood up and stay close to me," Alita ordered, picking up the pace. I drew my hood up over my curly hair, hunched my shoulders, and set out right on her heels. I couldn't imagine why such secrecy was necessary in a brightly lit hallway, but once again, I didn't dare question her orders since I had seen the things she was capable of. Soon Alita stopped in front of a doorway and sighed.

"Act normal," she whispered, then she flung the door open. I couldn't see into the room since I had stopped short of the actual doorway.

"Guess who I found?!" she cried with what I thought was fake happiness. I rolled my eyes. She tugged on my arm, and at first I didn't realize she intended for me to go through the door. She yanked harder, literally pulling me into the room. I lost my balance and almost landed on one knee, but Alita grabbed the back of my sweatshirt to steady me.

"Ta-dah!" she cried, throwing back my hood and exposing my face to the bright lights in the room. I took in the details rapidly—Alita's eager face, some tall blonde guy, and the person I was most glad to see: Liz.

Fourteen

Lianco

I observed the scene unfolding before me with conflicting emotions—heartfelt joy mixed with rueful agitation. Alita had gotten the one person we needed most, but by the looks of him, she had broken every rule of the code in doing so. I shot her a disapproving look, but she did not even glance in my direction. Liz and Dan were standing not three feet from each other, but neither one had moved. Liz stared in shock, eyes wide, her jaw hanging open.

"Dan," she whispered, as she slowly resumed her composure. Her other half raised his head slightly, glancing at me for a moment, before shifting his gaze over to his sister.

"Hey," he whispered back.

The tension in the room was palpable, the eerie silence filling the large space entirely. Liz looked concerned and a bit confused by her twin brother's complete lack of emotion. Then, she turned to me with narrowed eyes.

"What happened to him?" she asked flatly. "What have you done?"

I stole a glance at Alita, whose face bore no trace of remorse, only pleasure and pride.

"Your brother has had a long journey," I began. "You both could use some rest."

"*What?!*" Liz cried angrily. "Wait a minute. You said

you'd explain everything once Dan got here!"

"Now is not the time, nor the place. You need to rest."

"That is completely unfair!" Liz fumed.

"Look," Alita stepped toward Liz as she spoke, "your brother has been through a lot in the last ten minutes. He really could use some down time."

"And *you!*" Liz turned to fully face Alita. "Who are you anyway? You told me your name was Anna, right?"

Alita froze.

"Because this idiot over here called you Alita. I distinctly remember you telling me your name was Anna, and I never forget a name." Liz crossed her arms indignantly.

Without moving a muscle, Alita shot her thoughts at me. *So the old guy let something slip! Ha! This is your fault.*

I could not tell if Alita was delighted or frustrated from her tone, and, to her credit, her face had not changed one bit with her emotions.

"Liz," I cajoled, "I promise, no, I swear, we will explain everything later. In your current state, you would not absorb the information the way we want you to, the way we need you to. You have to trust that we know what is best right now."

Pacified for the time being, Liz gave in with a barely audible grumble and a nod. Rapidly I shot orders through *allreçu* to Darien and Orion to gather a team to prepare a room for our guests.

"Very good, then," I concluded. "This way please."

Alita opened the door and ushered out a very confused Dan. In a gesture of courtesy, I offered my arm to Liz, who looked appalled at my offer and walked stiffly past me, her arm brushing the doorframe in her haste. I sighed, knowing that many levels of trust had already been broken, and I had little idea how to earn them back.

Liz

The long hallway seemed to go on forever. The bright, fluorescent lights at the start transitioned to much softer lighting, which turned to lowlights, until we were walking in such dimness I could only see the outlines of the people in front of me. Four sets of footsteps echoed through the chamber-like walls, continuously reverberating down the hallway until they were too far away to hear.

I thought for sure we were going to walk until darkness completely engulfed us, but we stopped after a while. I couldn't see around Dan's massive shoulders, but I could hear feet shuffling that I knew were not part of our initial party. Dan's shape began moving forward once again, and I grabbed onto his sweatshirt so as to not be left behind. Feet shuffled and bodies brushed by each other until Dan, Lio, and I stood in front of a tall door, facing Alita and a couple of people I didn't recognize who were obviously waiting for us. The lighting had significantly improved so we could see them fairly clearly now.

The first person was a woman, whose silvery-blonde hair shone in the light. Her hair created a halo around her face and rippled down to her waist in pin-straight wispy lines. She was petite, a good six inches shorter than my tall frame. Her gray eyes watched me with curiosity and amusement, and a slight smile graced her lips.

The two men standing next to her were, at first glance, almost identical. However, a closer look revealed some distinct differences. The first of the men had medium length, jet-black hair; long enough that it swept across his forehead, but short enough that the black waves stayed off his shoulders. His hard, dark blue eyes stuck out from his rather exotic complexion. The other man had the same jet black hair, but cropped short and gelled into what could only be described as a miniature mohawk. His eyes were the same color as his hair, and even more menacing.

All three looked to Lio, then back to Dan and me.

"Greetings," the woman said formally in a soft, high-pitched voice. She inclined slightly as if to bow, and the other two followed suit. Slightly panicked by their formality, I glanced over at Lio, who gestured for me to bow in return.

"Um, hi," I said awkwardly, failing to pull off my bow with as much dignity and grace as the others had displayed. The blonde woman put out her hands in protest.

"Please, miss, you need not bow to us."

I hesitated, then returned to my full height.

"Miss?" Dan snickered beside me. "What are you, the queen?"

The woman opened her mouth but Anna/Alita intervened, stepping carefully between us.

"Allow me to introduce you," Anna said to us. "This is Ariana, Darien, and Orion."

The three of them bowed again, respectively, as their names were said.

"I'm Liz, and this is—"

"They know who you are," Anna interrupted me. The silver haired woman smiled engagingly, her long wisps of hair flying around her face. Dan was obviously still amused by the 'miss' comment, since I could feel his shoulders rocking in silent laughter. I jabbed him in the arm but that just seemed to make the whole experience even funnier to him.

I glanced over toward Lio, who was unusually quiet. He was just staring around the hallway at nothing, his gaze sometimes resting on a face, but mostly just wandering. I watched him carefully, curious as to what was going through his mind. I was still feeling the sting of his earlier fury. I couldn't imagine what might have happened had Anna and Dan had not barged in when they did.

"Well," Anna began, "now that we've done the official introductions, would you like to see your room?"

Sixteen

Dan

After I regained my composure, I casually wiped away the tears that had welled up in my eyes from holding back a giant laugh. I disguised the maneuver by passing a hand through my hair.

When I heard the faint mention of "our" room, I felt Liz stiffen beside me. I knew Liz better than I knew anyone, so I knew that maintaining her personal bubble was very important. I also knew from experience that Liz was a neat freak, pretty much the opposite of me, so sharing a room was not something she would enjoy. I raised my hand slowly, keeping my eyes on the floor so as to not offend my twin, or these new strangers, or even worse, start laughing again.

"Dan?" Lio asked.

"Yeah…um…I don't think the whole sharing a room thing is going to work for us."

"Who said anything about sharing a room?" Lio asked politely, resting his hand against the wall. I pointed at Alita.

"Uh, she did. She said 'your room.' That's not plural…"

"Well then, she should have been more specific. Why not take a look inside and see for yourself?"

I put one hand on the doorknob and paused. Lio gave me an encouraging smile and the door swung open silently. The place was amazing. The inside was a conglomeration of interesting styles; a mixture of medieval, modern, and rustic furnishings. It was considerably brighter than the hallway, a change I found very welcome.

Liz wandered in and around the room, her eyes wide, her fingers drifting over various objects in the room as though she was trying to absorb everything through her hands.

"Do you like it?" The soft, liquid-honey voice materialized beside me. The woman called Ariana was very small, but the new lighting gave away even more of her beauty. Her eyes were gray with tinges of ice blue, and they shone with delight at our obvious approval of the room. Her silver-blonde hair drifted behind her when she walked, even though the room was breezeless. It was like watching someone walk through water, only we were clearly on land. She caught me staring and smiled.

Seventeen

Lianco

My eyes followed Liz, who was slowly moving around the room, but my thoughts were elsewhere.

They like it, Alita sent. I nodded in response.

Alright, she demanded, *what's going on? You were fine about five minutes ago!*

Her thoughts passed through my head with the usual mockery and a degree of tenderness, but I did not even acknowledge them. I was too busy watching for changes in the layers of the Realm, specifically in the Unknown. I was also listening to the second stream of thoughts I was picking up. Like the first, the second odd stream of thoughts contained a lot of static, but there were words mixed in too. I could not quite catch them, but to focus more on that would distract me from my primary goal.

Watching the Unknown was like waiting for a fish to jump in a massive lake. You know one will jump, but you can not look everywhere at once, and you just know you will miss something if you look the wrong way. I struggled to concentrate, to keep my thoughts focused, but the layers of the Unknown began to vibrate, flinging themselves from side to side. I snapped out of my reverie, and prepared to sound an immediate alarm, when I felt a hand on my shoulder again, this time harder than before.

"Everything okay up there?" I could hear the smile in Alita's voice as she tapped the back of my head playfully with one finger. "You looked totally gone."

"Everything is fine," I reassured her. I also saw Ariana eyeing me in concern. My heart hurt to lie to her, but I smiled and waved a hand to let her know everything was all right.

"Well, then," I announced crisply, "now that you are settled, we will take our leave. There is sufficient food and drink here in the kitchen, and plenty of entertainment. You will find clean clothes in your rooms. We will return to you in the morning."

"Wait!" Liz called. "The morning? What about our classes? Our roommates?"

"Do not worry, Liz. Everything has been taken care of."

*   *   *

The five of us ran down the hallway. The walls flashed by at a dazzling rate of speed. The Alliance was a maze of corridors, rooms, and stairwells, all of which I was able to navigate easily, having roamed them for so long. They were designed like a maze for a purpose, to render the unwelcome helplessly lost. Only those who belonged were sure-footed and confident of their direction, even at this speed.

"How do you plan to explain all of this to them, Lianco?" Ariana inquired softly. I shook my head, indicating my reluctance to discuss the subject. I heard Alita sigh loudly, and braced myself for whatever she might add. Thankfully, before she could say anything, we reached my office.

"There is someone I would like you all to meet," I said as I opened the door.

Eighteen

Alita

Lianco opened his office door so slowly I thought I would die from suspense. My natural impatience started to take over, and I imagined the Earth crumbling into pieces, with me still waiting for him to get that damn door all the way open. But what I saw inside was more shocking than anything I could have imagined. The girl who waited for us stood up and smiled with a row of perfect teeth.

"Hello, Violet," Lianco said evenly. I thought I was going explode. The perfect honey blonde waves, the crystal blue eyes, those teeth, the stunning figure—I knew exactly who she was.

"Bitch!" I shrieked, lunging at her. She stepped back in alarm, her mouth in a perfect little "O." Ariana and Orion grabbed my arms as I struggled to get closer to her.

"What the *hell* is she doing here?" I snapped.

"Alita, please!" Lianco didn't even bother to send me thoughts, he just barked the words harshly in an effort to stop me.

"Violet? I don't think so. That...is Brooke," I growled. I could not believe he would dare to bring her here. Of all the people in the world, he had the most infuriating one sitting in the comfy chair in his office. I couldn't even begin to fathom why she would be there in the first place, so even restrained as I was, I whipped my head around to find out.

"Yes, that is Brooke," Lianco said gently.

"What is she *doing* here?" I managed to make my voice toneless, even though I was practically boiling over with anger.

"Alita, how do you know her?" Lianco asked. "Where is all of this anger coming from?"

"She's in all of the same classes as Liz and me. She's a conniving, cheating, lying whore who shouldn't be allowed anywhere near here!" I could barely control my voice. "So, tell me, why is she here?"

"She is in all of your classes because she has been involved in an undercover operation for the last five years. That is also why you have never seen her here before."

"Undercover operation?" I repeated, confused. "That sort of thing hasn't been done in ages. And that's Roku business anyway!" I was seething, shocked that someone like her would turn out to be one of us.

"Generally, yes, the Roku sector deals with that line of work," Lianco continued, "but they made a special exception in this case."

"The Roku? The Roku made an exception?" This was more than I could handle in one day. "They would never take someone who was not their own. What's so special about *her?*" I pointed at Brooke, who instantly opened her mouth to respond. Lianco cut her off before she could throw an insult back at me.

"Alita, she is a special case. Kind of like us."

"How special?"

"I'm a Reiku," Brooke, or Violet, interjected, obviously annoyed at not having been able to get a word in before. "I'm part Seiku and part Roku. Lianco created the name."

I almost dropped dead on the floor. To be part Seiku and part Roku was physically, mentally, and by all aspects of the Realms, virtually impossible. There was no way two people from such incompatible sectors, the two with the longest history of enmity since the beginning of time, could come together to have a child. Before the Alliance, the Rokus and the Seikus were in constant warfare. Their fighting caused the humans around them to fight with each other as well. Some of the most horrible wars and rulers in ancient times were influenced by one of the two groups, or a combination of both.

Such deep and lengthy hatred did not leave room for a personal relationship. It just wasn't possible. I could feel the others around me recoil as well once they processed her words. Ariana let out an audible gasp. In our experience, the only joint child the Alliance had ever known was Lianco. There had been no one else. Now, the girl I hated with a passion was more special than me, and almost as special as the leader of the whole freaking Alliance. As a group, we could not help but stare at her.

"So that means she has the power of both sectors?" Ariana carefully asked from behind me.

"Yes, both Seiku and Roku run in her veins," Lianco replied, as casually as he could. "She is like me."

This can't be possible, I sent at him.

But it is.

Out of the corner of my eye, I could see Brooke was agitated. She fidgeted with her hands and shifted her weight back and forth, obviously uncomfortable with being scrutinized so closely and judged so harshly. Her eyes flicked around angrily at all of us. Prepared to take full advantage of the situation, I turned toward her.

"You got something to say?" I asked menacingly.

"No," she shot back quickly. Secretly, I was impressed at her self-control, but outwardly I merely shrugged and turned back to Ariana.

"It's just, you all are talking about me like I'm not even here!" she suddenly cried. I smiled dangerously and turned back to face her.

"Well, what I want to know is why were you around Liz for the last four years? And why are you here now? Why are you in *all* of my classes?"

"What do you mean?"

"I mean, what were you doing living the happy, peppy cheerleader life in the same small town as Liz? And how is it you end up at the same exact college as her, when it's almost 500 miles away from that little town? Seems a little too coincidental, don't you think?"

She rolled her eyes and shrugged, as though my questions were not important enough to be answered.

"Ask him," she said with the sarcastic tone I knew so well, as she pointed a slim finger at Lianco.

Nineteen

Lianco

Alita whirled on me. Her eyes were on fire, her mouth as flat and slim as a crack in a stone wall. *Fire and brimstone…how ironic*, I thought to myself. I almost chuckled but was snapped out of my little daydream by a blinding pain. I reacted by putting my hand to my cheek, gingerly touching a sensitive spot where I knew a bruise would later emerge if not attended to. Alita stood in front of me, one hand still clenched into a fist. Her whole body was shaking. Everyone around us was in shock. Ariana moved toward me, raising a hand to comfort or console, but I put up a finger to stop her.

Hey, I sent quietly.

I…I…I… Alita was floundering, even in her thoughts.

You throw a wicked punch.

A snort came from an ashamed Alita. "I'm sorry," she murmured aloud. "Sometimes I just—"

"I know."

She unfolded her hand and put it gently to my face and winced, as though she could feel the pain she had caused. There was a slight sparkle in the corner of her eye, but if it was a tear, she wiped it away before anyone else could see.

"Well," Brooke interjected, "aren't you going to ask him?"

Alita threw a scornful glare at Brooke before turning back

to face me. "Is this part of the undercover crap? Did you have something to do with her being involved in Liz's life?"

I smiled at her vulgarity. She was back to her bossy, indignant self. "Yes, I did."

"Why? Why was she needed?" Alita looked forlorn, as if the world she thought she knew so well was not really what she thought it was.

"I am happy to explain the rest of the story, but everyone should sit down first," I announced.

"Are we going to have story time?" Brooke said sarcastically, a withering smile stretched across her beautiful face.

"Something like that…"

"*Supellex*," I murmured. The spare chairs flew out of their portals in the walls of my office and arranged themselves in a circle. Everyone seated themselves and looked to me.

"We first discovered Brooke's unique abilities during her qualifying test," I began. Brooke grinned broadly, shining in the attention, but Alita glared at her until she stopped. "She had been trained as a Roku in the Lampeon squadron, the elite female fighting force in the Roku sector. Most of you know that the Lampeon squadron has a very high bar for membership. Because Lampeon blood was in two of her past generations, her mother's and grandmother's, Brooke was selected for this training at the unusually young age of four. Realize that this is at least ten times younger than the normal qualifying age. Her mother, Gwennyn, served as an active Lampeon squad member for over 45 years. Brooke's father is a mystery, since no one ever came forward to admit fatherhood. Even her mother could not remember the father of her child very well.

"Brooke's magical ability was discovered during her final qualifying test. I am always invited to attend the final testing by the Lampeoni, the leaders of the squadron and part of the qualifying panel for all of Roku. During the final of five tests, Brooke was disarmed by the giant she faced. However, before he could cut off her hand with his immense axe, purple sparks shot out of her fingertips to weave a crude shield. The shield held off her opponent's weapon long enough for her to dart through his legs, retrieve her own weapon, and end the battle. Of course, the Roku leaders could not see the shield; those who are not Seiku cannot see magic unless that Seiku wishes it to be so. The Rokus were ecstatic that Brooke defeated a fearsome opponent with such skill and a quick recovery. At the time, even I could hardly see the shield, but my Seiku abilities enabled me to recognize there was magic. After she received congratulations from the qualifying panel, Brooke received her Roku sector marking."

Each of them looked down at their own left wrist involuntarily. All Alliance members are given a mark upon completion of their qualifying test, to symbolize their official membership in the Alliance and to indicate which sector they belong to. The mark is an ink insignia made upon one's left wrist, and each sector's insignia is unique. The marks grant passage to and from the Alliance, kind of like having a key. They are designed to keep the enemy out and the untrained in. Receiving one's brand is a painless process, but it is highly regarded as a rite of passage and a huge step forward for young members of the Alliance.

"Once they were marked, the new Rokus were taken to be given their names. None of them understood at the time how the naming process actually works, since the Book of Names is always kept under high security. All they knew was that one's name was already chosen by the Book, and when you were allowed into its chamber, your given name would already be printed on the open page. Thus, the anticipation surrounding the naming process was tremendous. Just as all of you were warned once, each of the inductees who came in contact with the Book was strongly advised against touching it."

The one person in the history of the Alliance who dared to touch the Book of Names was a boy named Thorn, a Seiku. He had tried to flip through the pages of the Book to locate the names of his friends. When the chamber was opened, all they found of Thorn was a pile of smoking ashes. Since then, the name Thorn has never come up in another naming ceremony.

"All of you have entered the chamber so you know what it is like. When Brooke entered the chamber, the name on her page spelled out:

"The Roku leaders assumed, naturally, that the name Violet was given because of her eyes, which are the strange purplish-blue that you see before you." Violet preened and flipped her hair. "At the time of her naming, only I realized it also had to do with her Seiku bloodline. As Orion can tell you, each Seiku has a power color that becomes visible when their magic is performed. Other Seikus can see a young trainee's power color, but as their power grows, Seikus develop the ability to hide it. Once they attain a certain level of strength, their power color is completely invisible.

"Seiku members hide their magic and colors so well that someone outside the Seiku sector would not even know magic was being performed. Even to the trained eye, all one would see is flashes of white light, unless the Seiku wishes his or her power to be known. Violet's power color happens to be the same as her name, which is both a blessing and a curse. One of us would recognize her power immediately, but so would a trained enemy.

"I confronted Violet about the possibility of dual powers after she received her name. She admitted that she had been surprised at the appearance of the shield in her battle. She told me she did not know who her father was, so I immediately sent her to a beginner Seiku class. Master Kailen scoffed at the idea of having a marked Roku in his class because of the deep hatred between the two sectors. After much persuasion on my part, however, he complied. It appears that accepting her was a good choice, since the Master admitted after only one class that he felt more magical energy from Violet than from any other student. She was immediately put into an advanced Seiku training course, in addition to the requirement of maintaining her regular Lampeon workouts.

"So she's like a double trainee?" Alita interjected.

"No longer a trainee," I replied. "She has completed all of her training and is a full Alliance member in both the Seiku and the Roku sectors."

Brooke displayed her left wrist proudly, where both the Roku and Seiku marks gleamed in the office light.

"But that doesn't explain her being around Liz," Alita argued.

"I have not gotten to that yet, Alita. Patience, please."

"Oh, right," Alita looked a bit defeated, but she masked her disappointment and glared at the wall so no one could see her embarrassment.

"We all know that once a name is given, it disappears back into the Book once more. The next week when the Neku in charge of protection and upkeep of the Book went for the daily inspection, Violet's name was still written on the page. And underneath it was written:

Protect the Legends

"The Neku keepers sought me out, as Alliance leader, and showed me the words from the Book. Once I read them, they instantly disappeared, like water through a strainer. Both of us were shocked, as this type of occurrence is unprecedented in current knowledge. That is when we decided to go through the Archives in the Neku sector to look for any mention of who or what the Legends might be. We searched for days but found nothing, no sign or reference to anything known as the Legends. I stayed as long as I could before returning to run the Alliance, but Guana kept looking."

"Guana? Guana helped you look?" Ariana asked tentatively. She was reluctant to interrupt, but her shock spurred her to speak up.

"Yes, Guana was a tremendous help," I said.

"But she hardly ever comes out of that little room at the back of the Neku!"

"Well, I do not know why you say that. She jumped into action as soon as I mentioned it to her, stating that it was her right as the Neku Master to oversee the search."

Ariana's cheeks reddened with embarrassment.

"Anyway," I continued, "Guana kept looking for any sign or mention of the Legends. She searched page after page of every book in their library. We had basically given up until there was a remarakable discovery. One of the Neku members saw a faint glow under the floorboards in a dilapidated storage room. When the boards were removed, a shallow hole was discovered. Buried in the hole was the ancient Book of Rokenan, held for centuries in its own personal crypt. The Book was so rotten and moldy that the pages were barely turnable." I grinned. "And that is where we found the answer."

Liz

I stood at the counter, eating peanut butter straight from the jar. Twirling the spoon lazily in my fingers, I stared aimlessly around at the apartment that was temporarily ours. Dan was pacing back and forth across the room like a madman. He would pound all the way to one wall, then stop, sigh, turn, and stomp back to the other wall.

"How can you stand there so calmly?" he demanded. Dan paused to glare at me for a few seconds, shook his head, and then resumed his pacing. "I mean, how can you just stand there and eat peanut butter like that?"

"You mean with a spoon?" I teased.

"Ha," he said without a hint of a smile. "I mean so calmly! Aren't you the one who always freaks out about stuff like this? I don't freak out, that's not me!"

I chuckled quietly at the humor of the situation. He was right. Usually I was the one who had a fit over the circumstances of whatever trouble we found ourselves in. But despite the fact that I currently loathed him, for some unexplainable reason I trusted Lio. I knew we weren't going to be hurt. We just had to wait. Meanwhile, there was a stocked refrigerator, a pantry filled with food, and a whole wall of bookshelves filled with books. I was content for the time being, and instead of me, Dan was the one freaking out.

"Ugh!" he said angrily. "I just don't get it! And stop laughing!"

I raised my eyebrows and looked at him innocently.

"You know what's weird?" he asked, finally coming over to the counter where I stood.

"What?"

Dan took his time to reply. His long finger snaked its way past my spoon into the jar of smooth peanut-y goodness. I rolled my eyes.

"Hey, 'tard, what's weird?" I asked, pushing his shoulder.

"The girl who brought me here…Alita, I guess? She took me through some kind of door in what looked like a solid brick wall. But it wasn't a door, really, she made it a door. It was a door made of light or something."

"A door made of light…right…"

"I'm serious! I think this whole place is odd like that. Doors made of light, long empty corridors, creepy lighting, weird people…it's like something out of a Harry Potter book!"

My thoughts wandered to the popular fictional character whose adventures in magic had earned his creator millions of dollars in book sales. But that was just fiction. Magic and doors made of light only existed in fantasy books. This was the real world.

"You can't be serious," I said as I took another spoonful of peanut butter.

"I'm being totally serious!"

"Dan, you've got to trust them. Honestly, …"

"God! You never listen to me," he whined. My head whipped around and my eyes locked onto his. He realized what had happened and put two hands up in surrender.

"Sorry, I forgot," he said apologetically. Dan knew for a fact that the one thing I hated the most in the entire world was whining. I couldn't stand it. The high pitched voice, the nasally drone, the pouty face; whining was nauseating.

"It's okay. Don't worry about it. Believe me, I also want to figure out what's going on, but pacing and worrying won't help us get to an answer."

"I told you. This place is weird, and mystical, and—"

"Dan! That's enough. Give it a rest, will you?" But even as I spoke the words, I began to wonder just how I had gotten into this weird place—I *had* been unconscious.

Dan

I lay in bed, staring at the ceiling, trying to tune out the soft snores coming from the room on the opposite side of the apartment. The place itself was fantastic, complete with a large, flat screen television, a full surround-sound stereo, every CD imaginable, and all the books Liz could ever hope to read. But whoever created this apartment had obviously put no thought or consideration into sound-proofing the walls.

Liz had always snored. At home, she was sometimes so loud I had to plug my ears with my iPod earbuds to drown her out. The walls of the house we grew up in were paper-thin; only a slim sheetrock wall separated our headboards. I could always hear Liz's snores loud and clear. Here, an entire apartment separated our rooms, but I could still hear her. In a way, it was comforting to be around her and her sleep noises again, but on top of everything else, the snoring was incredibly annoying.

Maybe it was because we were twins, but arguing was as natural for Liz and me as eating. It was a little weird that we hadn't argued in months. But, attending different colleges had separated us, so although we did talk on the phone a couple of times a week, we had not had any face to face conversations. Liz and I had always been close, but the last few months had made it harder to keep that bond, given the physical distance between us. That was one positive thing about this whole situation. Liz and I would get more time together, but I still had my doubts about these people and their motives for keeping us here.

Twenty-Two

Lianco

Protect the Legends. Those three words were my only instructions. But what did they mean? No one had even known of the Legends' existence until their story surfaced that day. Every sector in the Alliance had an ancient book, which chronicled and described the details of their people, from their origins and development all the way through present day. Each book was carefully protected and kept in pristine condition in the very center of the Neku Archives. But one had been forgotten. The Book of Rokenan had been hidden under the floorboards when we found it, buried in an ancient cavern and covered by layers of dust.

Before the discovery, I had only heard the Rokenan mentioned once before, in a bedtime story my mother, Nephy, used to tell me. According to the story, the Rokenan had tried to take control over the other sectors, and the others did not appreciate the attempt at conquest. In response, the Alliance had banded together and taken the necessary steps to rid the world of all Rokenan souls. It made for a fantastic bedtime story; however, I was never convinced of its accuracy and wanted to discover, even at a young age, the true story behind the children's tale.

Guana discovered the answer to my long-held question after some in-depth research in the Book of Rokenan.

According to her findings, the Rokenan had been the most powerful sector in the Alliance. They possessed the abilities of all four sectors: Leku, Seiku, Roku, and Neku. In other words, they had had almost infinite power, and truly could have been conquerors, but they had remained faithful to the Alliance for centuries. The book made no mention of desires to rule over the Alliance.

The Book of Rokenan also detailed a fateful battle, in which a Seiku and a Rokenan had gone head-to-head in a battle of skill. Not surprisingly, the Rokenan warrior won.

Since the battle lacked witnesses, the Seiku warrior told everyone that the Rokenan had cheated, and that the fatal wound in his side was the fault of his opponent. In reality, the Rokenan had obeyed the rules and stuck to using only his Seiku powers. He had won the match fair and square. The disgruntled Seiku's wound had been self-inflicted as a result of a careless miscalculation.

The man's lie, and subsequent death, seemed to be the final straw in a collective escalation of jealousy within the Alliance. The other four sectors rose up against the Rokenan, and, by banding together, succeeded in wiping them from the face of the planet. Just before his death, the last remaining Rokenan, a man by the name of Trian, had written the final entry in the Book of Rokenan.

It took Guana almost a week to decipher what she could from Trian's passage, mostly due to the deteriorating condition of the book's pages. Despite her best efforts, she could only restore pieces of the passage. The rest of the book was in shambles and would take days to recover, even with all of her golems working together. Guana pieced together the entry page as much as possible, and what was written was grim indeed.

What a grave time for us. Everyone is gone. Everyone is dead. Women, children, elders, no mercy was shown. I have seen evil - stared it in the face - and it is terrifying how jealousy can ruin the best of men! How envy turns a man's heart black with greed! I have seen my loved ones burned, hanged and dismembered they use whatever methods they can to get rid of us. Nothing stops them. I know my time is coming, my time to write is running out. I can only hope that someone will see this one day, I pray it will not go unnoticed

the Book had a message. Do Not Fear, the Legends will come.

they will be of our kind. Rokenan will rise again. the kindest

will be back to deliver the alliance from the hands of the enemy when they are needed most

The last word was stretched out, and the most disturbing thing of the whole passage was the drop of blood at the bottom. We assumed Trian was found as he was writing, since his last word remained unfinished and his blood was spattered onto his prophesy. But how the sacred book of a detested and eradicated sector managed to survive was still very much a mystery.

After several hours of experiments and the discovery of Neku fingerprints, Guana shared her hypothesis regarding the book's survival. She suggested that some wise Neku had reasoned that it would be best to hide the Book of Rokenan in an effort to preserve the knowledge it held. No doubt this person had acted quickly, perhaps even secretly, and placed the book under the library floor after Trian's death, hoping it would somehow survive. And so it had. After so many years, the book had collected enough dust and mold to rot the pages and render it almost useless in the hands of anyone but Guana. We were indebted to her restorative skills.

The mysterious Book of Rokenan foretold the Legend's existence, and expected us to find them. We had indeed found them, but the Book could not tell us why they were needed; too many pages were unreadable. So the question remained: why exactly were Liz and Dan needed and how could we possibly explain it to them?

Twenty-Three

Liz

The night is cool and dark, the air so moist I can reach out and watch small droplets appear on my hand. I walk alone, down the sidewalk at school, each footstep echoing across the courtyard and bouncing back to fill my ears with its emptiness. I walk past the library into the thicket of trees, the leaves rustling as I pass. I pause at the side of the building, a glowing doorway fills my view. Though it glows, the door appears solid and opaque. It is made up of the bricks of the building, but they emit a distinctly blue glow. I tentatively put my hand on one of the bricks and it disappears inside, reappearing when I pull my hand back out. I take a breath and throw myself against the wall, but I don't hit anything. Instead, I find myself inside a stone corridor. The hallway seems endless; the torches lining the walls grow dimmer in the distance until they disappear entirely. I know this corridor, this feeling, this place. But, I can't think how I know it.

There is a figure up ahead, a girl with long silvery hair. She turns toward me, the torch light bouncing off her gray eyes and her shimmering hair. She reaches out one hand and beckons me to come forward as a coy smile spreads across her face. I start to move, recognizing that the girl is Ariana. In a few long steps, I reach her, my hand already stretched out to grasp hers. But, before I can touch her, she disappears, breaking apart into tiny pieces like dust in the wind.

I spin around a few times, puzzled, before I see another figure appear farther down the hallway. It's Serenu. His dark, wavy locks cover the menacing eyes that I so clearly remember from that night in the Quad. When I finally reach him, poised to strike, he disappears as well, blown away in the single blink of an eye. I cry out, infuriated that I cannot reach anything. I break into a sprint, charging down the hallway as if my life depends on it. Up ahead, I see Dan in his basketball uniform, Lianco with a smile playing across his lips, Alita with a book in her hand, and all them disappear just as I get to them. I call out to each, but there is no response. No sound. Suddenly I'm running down an empty corridor. No one is waiting for me. The hall is endlessly long, the torches rushing by as I sprint faster and faster. I see a light, just a tiny hint of light, at the end of the hall.

The small glint gets closer and closer, but no bigger. I can't tell what it is until I am close enough to see there is a mirror right in front of my nose. The glass is gigantic. I wonder why I couldn't see it from farther away. Then I notice the mirror is different than most, for I have no reflection. Nothing stares back at me, just an empty piece of glass. I see a figure appear in the mirror, a tiny person far away but getting closer every second. She is walking in a hall similar to mine, only hers is silver and brightly lit. She gets closer, and bigger, until she is standing right in front of me. To my surprise, she is me. There's my face, reflected back...but then again, not reflected, more like duplicated. It's not the real me.

As I watch, my other face begins to melt away until I find

I am staring at Brooke. She laughs joyfully, almost triumphantly. Her mouth moves but I cannot hear her. Then she points to my face and laughs directly at me. I look away, trying to escape the feeling of humiliation her laughter invokes, but she is everywhere. She is all around me, laughing and laughing. I turn back to the original and bang my fists against the mirror, screaming at her to stop. She laughs once more and puts her hand to the mirror. When she does, the mirror begins to crack. I close my eyes as shards of glass fly out toward me...

A slight push on my shoulder jarred me out of my nightmare. Clear gray eyes stared down into mine.

"Are you awake?" Ariana asked quietly in her high voice. I sat up and rubbed my eyes fiercely, trying to erase the sleepy layer and the memory of the bad dream.

"Yeah, I'm awake," I grumbled.

"Lianco has requested your presence."

"Who?"

"Lio," she corrected herself.

"Oh!" I jumped out of bed so quickly that I unintentionally smacked her face with my shoulder in the process. I apologized as I rapidly pulled on some clothes. I walked out of my room to find that Dan and Orion were already waiting in the living area, and Dan's eyes were clouded over with fatigue.

"Sleep well?" I asked casually, attempting to smooth down a few of the curls that were sticking up in different directions all over his head.

"Don't even start with me..." he replied with a scowl.

"This way," Ariana said evenly, as she ushered us out of the room.

*   *   *

We ended up in an office-like space no more than three minutes later, breathing hard and somewhat dazed from the trip. With Ariana in the lead and Orion on our heels, the speed at which we traveled was unbelievably swift. Dan and I had to sprint to keep up with their easy, long-strided run.

"Where are we?" I asked breathlessly.

"His office," Ariana replied. Her breathing was perfectly normal, while Dan and I were panting like horses at the end of a race. I looked in wonder at the area around us. It was sort of gothic, with high stone walls, a large fireplace in the center, and lots of oversized antique furniture. It looked like something you might see in a museum about the Middle Ages.

My head was tilted back, studying the grandeur of the high walls, so I missed Lio's entrance completely. With his usual grace, he silently appeared right beside me to welcome us. As he invited us to sit down, I thought how eerie it was that he could come and go like that. Maybe there was some truth to what Dan had said about magic doors.

"I know that you, Liz, have been especially eager for the information you are about to receive," Lio began. "Let me warn you, however, what I am going to tell you may not be shared with anyone outside of yourselves and the people in this Alliance. No other human souls may hear this. Ever. Do you understand?" He looked pointedly at Dan and me. Even in our sleep-deprived state, we both nodded solemnly. We were about to get some answers about the strange situation we had somehow gotten ourselves into. I, for one, was dying to hear Lio's explanation.

"Good," he said, taking a deep breath. "First, you should know that my name is not Lio. That was the name my mother gave me at birth. My true name is Lianco; that is, Lianco is the name the Book gave me."

"What's the Book?" I blurted out as my right hand simultaneously shot up in the air like an overeager student sitting in the front row in class. All heads turned toward me, but no one spoke. From their expressions I realized I had made an obvious mistake in etiquette. Ariana, who was seated on my right, reached up and gently pulled my hand down out of the air. She carefully placed it back on the couch, patting it twice for good measure as my cheeks burned with embarrassment.

"The Book is the law. It is everything. That might be hard for you to understand since you have nothing like it in your culture. Here in the Realm, we know that when the Book gives a message, which it rarely does, we must accept that message no matter what. It is this same Book that gives you your true name, Liz. You know yourself as Liz, because your parents named you that, but that may not be what the Book of Names has chosen for you."

Lio, or Lianco, as we were apparently supposed to call him now, proceeded to explain to us about some prophet who wrote in yet another book, (not to be confused with THE Book), about some people called the Rokenan. He spoke rapidly, filling our heads with as much information as he could in a short time. By the way he gestured as he spoke, I assumed that the Rokenan he was referring to could only be us, me and Dan. There was also something about a guy who died, a Neku-something, I think, but the most important part was still whatever was in the Book. We were going to go see it, which meant we were going to get our true names.

*   *   *

Before we could begin to process this new information, we were encouraged to stand up and follow. From another door in Lianco's office, we stepped into a corridor that was solid stone from top to bottom. Torches lined the walls as far as the eye could see and shadows danced around their light. I shrank into Dan's side as we walked, Lianco leading and the others flanking us.

"Scared?" he teased. I nodded and moved even closer toward him. The hallway looked like the one in my vivid dream. That memory, and my extreme fear of scary movies, took over my imagination. The long hallway could have easily passed for a monster's hideout, and murderers could lurk around the next corner, waiting to pounce on unsuspecting people. Or, maybe we'd come upon a non-reflecting mirror...I trembled slightly, praying for the hallway to end. We walked for a few minutes more until the corridor widened into an alcove on the right. In the middle of the alcove was a large, ornate wooden door.

"So far," Lianco began, "you have only heard about our history, that of the past and that in the making; who we are and where we come from. Through this door is the Book of Names, and only those who are welcome may enter. This is where we find out who you truly are."

He gestured to the door and everyone stepped out of our way. Ever the brave one, Dan reached out and grasped the knobby wooden handle. The door swung open easily, despite its size. The room inside could only be described as a castle chamber, like something I would read about in a fairy tale. The walls were the same stone as the corridor, but somehow they seemed older. It occurred to me that perhaps just one touch would send them crumbling to dust, and us with them. The room was not large, but its shadowy lighting made it seem cavernous. As I glanced around, I noticed it was perfectly round and symmetrical. The only light came from a lamp hung in the center, above a podium where a huge, leather bound book lay open. A man of purpose, Dan strode right for the podium.

"Stop!" I cried suddenly. Dan turned with a quizzical look.

"Why?"

"What if there's a trap or something?"

"A trap...really Liz?" he smirked. "I think you've read too many mystery novels. Or has your fear of dark and scary places gotten the better of you?"

I sighed and rubbed my temples. "Fine. Be my guest, walk to your death. I am staying *right here.*"

He continued up the three steps to the podium, but he was moving a little slower than before. I smirked at the thought that my childish fears might have infected him, too.

"Liz! Check this out!"

Unsettled by the bouncing echoes, I ran up beside him in a flash, running to escape monsters my imagination was inventing behind me. When I reached the top step I was in full view of the Book. It was magnificent, and clearly so old that it should have disintegrated by now. The inside of the Book had yellowed to the tint of old teeth, but there was not a single tear or fray on any of the pages. In the center of the left hand page, a single word began to appear.

Zoran

"How did..." I breathed.

"Whoa...this thing knows my childhood nickname!"

"But how?"

"I don't know, but that rocks!" Dan was grinning from ear to ear.

I was in shock. When we were young, Dan had created an imaginary friend named Zeke. Zeke was our constant companion. He accompanied us on every adventure. But Dan got upset one day that his imaginary friend had a better name than he did. I had laughed at his frustration, but had suggested he take the name Zoran so I wouldn't have to hear about it anymore. From then on, it was Zeke and Zoran to the rescue, Zeke and Zoran save the world, Zeke and Zoran on safari. But these names were secret. The only people who knew about them were Dan and I. We never told anyone else, not even our parents. To see that name again brought back a flood of memories. Truly, how could these Alliance people know about our childhood games? More importantly, how did the Book know?

I ran my fingers over the brilliant calligraphy, the swirls and etches of the letters were mesmerizing.

"Hey! Look!" Dan pointed at the Book again. On the opposite page, another name had appeared in the same beautiful letters.

Zaria

I gasped.

"Wow! This thing is really good," Dan exclaimed, with his arms flailing enthusiastically. "First it nails me, and then it gets you! It's genius."

"Zaria? What the hell does the name Liz have to do with the name Zaria?"

"Mom never told you?" he asked. I shook my head and furrowed my eyebrows to show him that I had absolutely no idea what he was talking about. "See, when you were born, Mom and Dad were debating what to name you. They had already decided on my name, but they were split on yours. Dad was pushing for a more symbolic or exotic name for you. He scrolled through dozens of books and finally suggested Branwen or Zaria. Mom, however, wanted a more traditional name. She was pushing for Meghan and Elizabeth. Dad was powerless—you know how stubborn Mom can be. Dad eventually gave up and they named you

Elizabeth, Liz for short."

"How come I've never heard this story?"

"Well, I'd never heard it until this summer. You were off at some leadership conference and I was bored, so I asked mom some questions about when we were born. You know how much mom loves to talk."

I snorted, envisioning my mother relating the story in a tender, heartfelt way to an otherwise bored, and extremely ADD, Dan.

"What?" he asked.

"Oh, nothing, I'm just surprised you heard the story before me. That's all."

"Well, now we know our names. Is that supposed to tell us who we are?"

"I don't know," I sighed.

"I mean, not that this isn't cool and everything, but all this does is give us new names. Kind of a rip-off, huh?" He threw his hands up in frustration and then slammed them down on the Book.

"Be careful!" I hissed and slapped his hand like I was his mother. He didn't even register that he'd heard me or felt my slap. He was looking down, staring at where the Book was suddenly writing new words.

"The L-E-wait is that a G?" he spelled.

"Yes, G. What is going on?"

"E-N-D-S," he finished. "The Legends."

Twenty-Four

Ariana

Torches and stone walls. That's all I could see in either direction. It was fascinating, to be sure, but a little unnerving. As far as I knew, no one in Alliance history had been all the way to the end of the corridor, and very few had dared to go beyond the opening to the room that held the Book. There were rumors that the passageway led straight into the Unknown, though that seemed impossible as I stood there looking down it.

Lianco couldn't be still; he paced back and forth outside the door to the chamber. Pacing was one his favorite things to do. I had known Lianco for a long time, so I knew that moving back and forth was his way of tackling his nerves and mulling over difficult problems. Darien, Alita, and Orion stood against the wall opposite from me, looking bored and talking quietly. We could hear nothing from inside the chamber.

"Lianco," I said quietly, drawing him out of his trance-like state. He looked over toward where I sat against the wall, his eyes searching for my face in the dimness. "They'll be fine," I reassured him. That one strong hand snaked its way through his hair, another familiar habit. He strode over to the wall and dropped down beside me.

"I just wish I knew what was going on in there," he

whispered angrily.

"I know," I soothed. He sighed heavily and lowered his head onto my shoulder. I shifted, trying in vain to make my bony shoulder more comfortable for him.

"Don't worry about it," he chuckled.

"My shoulder or the chamber?"

"Both, I suppose," he sighed. "I forgot how nice this is."

"What? My bony shoulder?"

"No, Ariana, just being with you. It has been a long and difficult road, has it not?"

My mind wandered at his words, and a string of images from the past instantly flashed before my eyes. The field, a picnic, his hair, the trials, swords falling, the pain…I winced at that. The memory of the pain itself was enough to make me forget the rest. My hands clenched into fists, my anger as fresh at that moment as any time before. Lianco's hand found its way to mine.

"I am so sorry, you know," he whispered.

"So you've said."

"Yet that does not change what happened, does it?"

"No, it doesn't," I said softly, extracting my hand from his grip. He sighed and looked into my eyes, searching for something, some indication of acceptance within me. He looked hopeful.

"You know we could never fix it," I said.

"You do not have to do anything!" he argued. "It was not your fault. Let me fix it."

"We can never go back. All we can do is move forward."

Lianco sighed. His fingers played with the ends of my

hair. The silver strands twirled around tightly, only to be released once more.

"I miss your hair," he said quietly.

"Mmm?"

"I miss the color."

"Black? It's not that interesting of a color."

"Maybe not to you, but I miss your dark hair more than anything else. You were my raven. My raven with the beautiful eyes."

My hands trembled as he ran his fingers over my face, tracing the area around my once-green eyes. The incident we both remembered so well had resulted in a change of color for my eyes as well as my hair. My once radiant green eyes had changed to a rather dull gray, and I went from a head full of pretty black hair to a wispy silver mop. Lianco's fingers found their way to the thin scar that ran from the nape of my neck to the crest of my collarbone.

"I am so sorry," he whispered as I fought back tears. "I did not mean to bring the memories back."

He wrapped one arm around my shoulders, and pulled me into him. Sparked by such a wonderfully familiar position, warm memories flooded my head and my heart, and then I couldn't stop the tears.

Dan

"What the hell does that mean?" I wondered aloud. Liz just shook her head back and forth slowly, continuously tracing the letters with her finger.

The Legends

Those two simple words sprawled across the page underneath our new names. But what did they mean?

I have to admit, I liked my original name. Dan was a pretty great name. But Zoran? Sure, that was fun when we were kids, but we were almost 19 now. Older, more mature. A lot less "Zoran-ish."

"What I don't get is how this thing," I said, gesturing at the Book's open pages, "knew something so personal. Something nobody but us could know."

"And where did the letters appear from?" Liz asked.

"The letters on the page?" I questioned.

"Mm-hmm…" she responded, deep in thought.

"No idea…maybe it's like some fake magic drawing board. Or maybe, that guy Lianco is writing the words on a remote screen. You think that's possible?"

"I suppose that is possible, but I somehow believe the Book is real," she replied. "I also don't think any more words are going to appear, so we should go back the others."

We walked back down the steps toward the heavy door. I glanced around at the ancient walls, then turned back to look at the very mysterious Book. The lamp above it flickered briefly and then the whole room went completely dark. I mean, dark. I couldn't see my own hand. I grabbed for Liz's hand and ran for where I had last seen the door. Liz started to hyperventilate, muttering something about running in a dream. After some exploratory searching, my fingers connected with a handle and I wrenched the door open.

The first thing I saw was five surprised faces. Lianco and Ariana were seated against one wall, and his arms were around her in what looked like a lover's embrace. Ariana looked like she'd been crying. The other three were standing against the opposite wall, and it was apparent they'd been talking together in a group. Lianco was by my side immediately.

"Is everything all right? What happened in there?" I guess it was obvious something was wrong. No doubt my face reflected my panic at being caught in a pitch-black room. Liz was pale and muttering incoherently to herself, which was alarming. Ariana came to Liz's rescue and lowered her to the floor. "What happened?" Lianco demanded again.

"The Book was in there…and there were names…and then someone turned the lights out," I managed to choke out. Without another word, Lianco barged through the door we'd just exited. Alita followed close behind him.

"*Ignis!*" Lianco shouted. Fire burst out of the air and circled the walls, entirely illuminating the room from ceiling to floor. Alita gasped and all of the color drained from Lianco's already pale face. I followed their gazes to the source of their shock. The Book was gone.

Lianco

No. It was not possible. The Book could not have vanished. It absolutely could not be gone.

"No!" I shouted. The fire around the walls blazed higher with my anger.

"It's gone," Alita breathed in disbelief, standing beside me.

"It cannot be gone!" I shouted. I whirled around and searched every crevice with my eyes. Darien and Orion moved from their positions against the wall and stood on either side of me in battle ready mode. Six pairs of eyes stared at me expectantly.

"But it is," I admitted bitterly.

"Gone?" Ariana said as she came in, just now comprehending what had happened.

"Yes. Gone." I repeated.

"Gone where, boss?" Darien inquired.

"Taken. Stolen. Lifted. *Gone.*"

"Oh," he replied hollowly.

"Do we...do we know who did it?" Ariana asked, her voice full of impending worry.

I looked around the room. A mixture of dread, anguish and doubt ran across the faces around me.

"I do," said a voice from behind us.

We all turned to confront the source of the voice. Violet stood in the corridor, purple magic radiating from around her hands.

"It was Serenu."

*   *   *

With Violet in tow, the eight of us flew down the corridor at our highest allowable speed, fear driving us to go more quickly than most had ever gone before. Liz rode on Orion's back, her curls rising and falling as he ran. Alita ran beside Dan, helping him, but only a little. Dan's natural athletic ability, aided by a small amount of his magic that seemed to be kicking in, allowed him to keep pace with the group. Darien brought up the rear, his acute senses on full alert and ready to detect unwelcome visitors.

Alita, I sent in mid-stride.

Mmm?

I need you and Orion to get Liz and Dan back to their apartment immediately.

Got it.

She dropped back to deliver the message, and the four of them took the next stairwell down, still moving at full speed toward their room.

"Are we headed to the Film?" Ariana asked me, not missing a beat.

"Yes. There is something we need to take care of."

I purposely had set my mind drifting, searching for any noticeable change in the layers of the Unknown. But from what I could tell, they remained as solid and as impenetrable as ever. Only one in the Unknown could truly see inside the Unknown.

"How do you know it was him?" I asked Violet. Still running at our break-neck pace, she turned her purple eyes to stare at me.

"I saw him. I saw him with the Book."

I glanced at Ariana, who nodded and sped up even more, though at this pace, the change was imperceptible. We reached the Film within a few minutes. As soon as I came into view, Logos stood at the entrance at full attention. As the head guard, he knew I needed to speak with him.

"Logos. I—"

"Sir!"

"Logos, I need you to be quiet and listen be—"

"Yes sir!"

"Shut up, pinhead!" Violet shouted.

I put a hand out to stifle Violet and poured all my attention into speaking calmly. "The Barrier has been broken. Your guards must be on full alert. I need to speak with all of them immediately."

Logos nodded and bowed his giant form over so that I could reach his head. As the leader of his kind, Logos had the telepathic power to send all the guards a message at once, much like our *allreçu* ability. By placing my hand against his temple, I could connect my *allreçu* with his ability and send my message out to the entire force. His skin was clammy with nerves, a purely physical reaction. His mind was also racing with questions, but I easily overcame his weak brain waves and began to speak.

Guards of the Alliance, this is Lianco. The Barrier has officially been penetrated. All portals must immediately be closed. Double the security on every entrance and contain anyone or anything that tries to escape. Effective immediately, no one leaves the Realm without my permission.

"Thank you, Logos." I managed some fraction of a smile.

"Of course, sir."

"Now, I need you to let me out."

"Yes, sir."

He released the Film and I moved forward to go through it. Three other bodies moved up beside me. I sighed and turned to them.

"I have to do this alone."

"You are not going out there by yourself," Violet declared. "If anyone goes, it should be me."

"Please, Lianco. You may need our help," Ariana pleaded.

"You're the leader, boss. You're kind of important. We can't afford to lose you," Darien agreed.

I hesitated, and then gave in after a moment. "Fine, but I am warning you to watch your backs."

We slipped through the Film and walked onto the grass that grew along the side of the campus library. I was not expecting sunlight, and after dwelling in the dimness of the Realm, the bright rays hit me with full force. The only unaffected one was Violet, who strode ahead resolutely, purple magic radiating in spheres around her hands.

"Serenu certainly timed this well," Ariana said.

Though she meant having us come out into the sunlight,

her response was even more accurate than she realized. I vaguely heard a bell ring, and abruptly students spilled out of doors all around us, almost filling the Quad. Violet stopped short, her magic dimming. She turned to me with a look of worry. Students were everywhere—on the grass, against trees, on the sidewalks. Any kind of magical disturbance on our part would not only scare them but also reveal us to them.

"Shit," I muttered. Timing was everything.

Twenty-Seven

Liz

Alita slid a mug of hot chocolate into my freezing hands, its heat already making a difference to my shivering body. The darkness in the chamber brought back the memory of those evil eyes that were so prominent in my dreams. I had panicked in the chamber and was suffering the consequences of the adrenaline rush. Dan sat on the couch in our borrowed apartment with my legs draped over his lap. One of his hands rested on my shin, the other was flipping through channels with the remote.

"Are you going to be all right?" Alita asked quietly.

"Yes," I smiled. "Thank you."

Somebody had pulled my mass of curls back into a messy bun. Due to the lack of a bobby pin, my overgrown bangs had flopped down over my face. I tucked them under the rest of my hair and grimaced.

"I need a serious shower, pronto."

Dan smirked. "What's the matter? Girl-stink doesn't suit you?"

"It's not that," I counter-smirked. "My hair and my clothes reek of smoke and oil from that hanging lamp. It's disgusting." I wrinkled my nose in distaste at my own body odor. "And, yeah, maybe I got a little sweaty when we were running for our lives." Dan looked to Orion, who was leaning against the wall.

"She okay to shower?" Dan asked.

Orion looked up and gave a single nod.

"You're good to go," Dan exclaimed. "Remember, lots of soap!" He threw my legs off his lap and gave me a little push toward the bathroom. I turned the water on hot and attempted to scrub off the various smells and the feeling of uneasiness that had come over me. I found several pieces of what appeared to be burnt ashes in my hair as I shampooed, though I wasn't quite sure how they got there.

When I finished, I wrapped a bath towel around my body and squeezed the extra water out of my hair. The luxurious, pure-white, fluffy towels were soft and warmed from the heat of the shower. I towel-dried my curls as best I could and wrapped them into a loose bun. It wasn't until I wiped the fog off the mirror that I saw the words. I whipped around to read them.

"The Legends will perish," I whispered aloud. The words were freshly written on the wall behind me in what appeared to be blood. Some of it was dripping down the wall in slow, horrible rivulets. I grabbed the sink to steady myself. My heart was pounding as I realized the Legends were Dan and me, and whoever wrote the message clearly intended to get rid of us. The dark, menacing eyes I was so familiar with swam into my vision. I tried to calm myself with a few deep breaths, which turned out to be more like ragged gasps. Those eyes, along with these awful words, burned deeper into my brain, and then I screamed.

Twenty-Eight

Lianco

Darien, Ariana, and I stood at the edge of the Quad not two feet apart from each other, unable to move. Violet was a few paces ahead, as frozen as we were. She searched our faces for answers to the million questions in her eyes.

What now? She mouthed at me. I was sifting through strategies at warp speed. If we launched any kind of real search, we would draw too much attention to ourselves. The student body was already wary of us. Although humans cannot actually see inner magic such as searching or discovery spells, they can, without question, feel its effects. Our magic causes them to feel unsettled and unstable, so their presence was inhibiting. We were going to need to do some serious magic to retrieve the Book. Plus, if any of us had to call on the elements to defend ourselves, it would be clearly visible to the students milling around us.

Well, well, Lianco. Aren't you in a dilemma? a voice sneered in my head. Surprisingly, I realized the voice was coming from the static, that second wave of sound I had been picking up in my head the last few weeks. My fists clenched with anger as my eyes rapidly scanned the area, looking for any sign of him.

I knew it had to be you.

Oh, how sweet, Serenu replied. *Little brother thinks he*

knows his big brother so well. His voice was teasing and dripping with sarcasm, as usual. *The problem is, you don't know me at all, you little runt.*

Come out and face me, I demanded.

Mmm, I could, but I don't want to upset all these people. You probably don't want me to upset all these people either since you live within their world. You're not in the Realm anymore. This is the human world, and you can't stop me here. I'll think I'll just disappear for awhile with my new Book.

The others were staring at me as my face changed expressions based on a conversation that only I was able to hear. They could tell I was speaking to someone through *allreçu*, but they had no idea who. Somewhere in the back of my mind, I was vaguely aware that a girl had subtly approached our group. I was too wrapped up in my mental conversation to pay any attention to others, and I knew Darien was watching closely and would take steps to protect me if the need arose.

The Book does not belong to you, you filth, I snarled.

Ah, that's where you're wrong, brother, Serenu answered. His voice had gone from dripping sarcasm to the embodiment of bitter hatred. *I have the Book, which means not only do I have the entire history of the Alliance in my hands, I hold its future as well. Surely you have realized I can write whatever I want in the Book. I can create the future I choose.*

His words took me by surprise, but I responded as if unfazed. *Don't be ridiculous. The Book's pages have not been written in since the Original Council. They are impossible to turn without the consent of the Book. Do you believe it will listen to you? Surely, the Book sees you clearly for who you are. Careful, it may just crumble in your fingertips...*

Maybe you're overlooking something, my naïve little brother, he laughed in my head. *Something such as the spell that controls the access to the Book.*

Serenu, no one has seen that spell in centuries.

Maybe, but where there's a will, there is definitely a way. I must leave you now, brother. I have an important meeting with my father.

I felt my blood grow still. If anyone knew the spell to access the Book, it would be Loki, Serenu's father. Loki's father had been a member of the Original Council, and thus, one of the creators of the governing spell. I thought Loki to be long gone, but Serenu spoke as if he were still alive. If what he claimed was true, it would mean Loki was the oldest living Being ever. It would also mean Serenu had access to Loki's knowledge and memory. Alarmingly, this news meant it was quite possible that all of us had a terrible fate ahead.

Twenty-Nine

Dan

I was flipping around the channels, wondering if it was possible to get any decent sports on television in the Realm, when suddenly an ear-piercing scream came from the bathroom. Alita was inside the door within seconds with me about three steps behind her. All I could see from where I stood were legs and a towel, which could only mean Liz was lying on the floor of the bathroom.

"Orion," Alita called over her shoulder. "I need you."

I stood completely still as Orion pushed past me into the bathroom and signaled me back toward the couch. My mind was racing at full speed, imagining a thousand scenarios for what may have happened. Low murmurs floated out through the open bathroom door, but I couldn't distinguish individual voices or understand what they were saying. I tried to settle myself by scanning around the room for anything unusual. My eyes dragged over the ancient walls that surrounded a fairly modern design. How we got sucked into this mess was a total mystery to me.

Liz was the strong one. The leader. It had always been that way. As for me? I had always been her 'charge' of sorts, definitely fulfilling the role of crazy twin brother. Liz traditionally took care of me in one way or another. It didn't matter if I treated her badly or said hurtful things; we had some kind of inborn connection that kept her coming back. She had stood by me through the gossip that always accompanied a break up and lost games that often turned the student body against me for a while. She was my strong, unwavering Liz…and now she was officially freaking out.

The realization was slowly dawning on me. Liz had always been my rock, and now it was my turn to do the same for her. I willed my feet to move closer to the bathroom until I was right in the doorway. Liz was sitting against the side wall with her eyes closed, nodding her head in response to the words whispered in her ear by Alita, who was crouched beside her. Orion faced the opposite wall, watching red-stained water trickle down the white wall in tiny rivulets. There were already watery red puddles on the floor. None of them noticed my presence.

When the last of the water had collected on the floor, Orion crouched beside the crimson puddles.

"*Ventus,*" he muttered. A slight breeze blew through the room, picking up the water particles as it went until there was nothing left on the floor. My jaw dropped at the display.

"How did you do that?"

"He's a Seiku," Alita answered without looking up.

"A what?"

"A Seiku," Orion replied. "One of the magic sector. A wizard, if you will."

"Wizard…?"

"Yes. I'm sure Lianco will explain the various sectors at some point," Alita interrupted. "He's kind of busy right now."

She turned her head slightly and concentrated on

something else, something we couldn't see. Her face moved as if expressing thoughts and she winced a little every few seconds. I turned back to Orion, but he had already stepped through the door back into the apartment where he was leaning against one of the walls with his eyes closed. Finally, I looked at Liz. She was not all right, that much was obvious. Her skin was waxy and pale, and her normally fantastic hair was in tangles around her shoulders.

"Is she going to be alright?" I said to Alita. "Shouldn't I take her to the clinic or something? I mean, she doesn't look good."

Alita shook her head slightly. "She will be fine in a little while. She had a bit of a shock."

Abruptly, a thought occurred to me, and I said, "Hey, how do people not notice we're missing? We've been gone to wherever this is for a while now. Don't our friends or teachers wonder why?"

"No, they don't wonder. We've got doubles of you who are going about your daily activities, one of you and one of Liz." She spoke so matter of factly, but surely she must have realized that kind of news would come as a shock to me.

"Doubles of us?" I managed to sputter out.

"Yes," she looked smug. "They attend all your classes, take your tests and go to any sports practices or meetings."

"Well, what about our roommates? I bet they can tell the difference in these doubles. They're probably suspicious already. What if they go to the police or something?"

"Your roommates don't have any problems with the doubles because we arranged for your schools to room you with Alliance members."

Her obvious enjoyment at shocking me was infuriating. It was time for me to take control.

"I have to get her out of here," I stated, my anger barely disguised. Without a word, Orion moved directly into the bathroom doorway, blocking my exit.

"With the current state of affairs? I don't think so," Alita countered.

"Look at her!" I said angrily. "She looks like she's going to pass out. I don't know exactly what's causing it, but I'm pretty damn sure it's got something to do with her being in this place!" My frustration had built until I was fuming, struggling to find the right words to express my anger.

"I'm sorry, but I can't let you take her," Alita said simply.

That was the final straw. I threw myself against the wall Liz was leaning on in a futile attempt to create another exit. She let out a surprised 'Oh!' as my fists connected with the solid structure. I banged against the wall as hard as I could until bits of skin and blood were sticking with each blow. I felt a cold hand on my leg and glanced down to see Liz looking up at me with her big, blue eyes.

"Don't, Dan." she whispered. "Please."

I collapsed beside her and laid my head on her shoulder. My hands were numb from the blows. Liz's hair was still wet from her shower and it dripped onto my forehead. She wasn't shivering anymore, but I could tell she was still terribly afraid.

"Are we all settled now?" Alita asked carefully. I glared up at her, trying to control my voice as much as possible.

"At least let her talk to my mom."

Thirty

Darien

It was happening again—one of those conversations inside his head that no one else could see or hear. Every sense in my body was on alert, tracking each sound, movement and smell in a two mile radius. That was the way of the Roku. We were trained from birth, raised to be terrifyingly alert and lightning fast. We were also trained in more sinister arts, like how to dismember a body in under three seconds and arrange it to look like an accident. We were deadly, and it was our greatest advantage. From day one, a Roku in training was taught to be in tune with all of the senses, and I had been fortunate enough to be born keenly sensitive. In training, it was discovered that I had the farthest-reaching abilities in all of Roku, which was how I got the position of being Lianco's escort. At first I was merely a 'soldier' assigned to guard and protect; as time went by, however, Lianco and I became friends.

Now I watched helplessly as my friend carried on what seemed to be a tormenting conversation within himself. This was not something I could help him with, or protect him from. All I could do was insure there was no outside threat, at least for now. As a fellow Roku, Ariana also stood poised to take action if necessary. I wondered if anyone else besides me had picked up on the relationship between the two of them. Their attachment was growing strong again, but it had been the most vibrant before the accident, before everything changed.

Lianco's head snapped up, and he stared across the student-filled Quad. I followed his gaze, but it seemed he was staring at nothing. Instinctively, my body went on full alert, to a level I had never felt before. Without asking, I knew Lianco was searching for rifts in the layers of the Unknown. Should anything come out of them and enter our Realm, I had to be ready immediately.

All at once, Lianco's head slumped against his shoulder and his knees buckled. Ariana's outstretched arms caught him before he could hit the ground.

"Is he breathing?" I asked, almost afraid to know the answer.

"He's breathing, but it's shallow," Ariana concentrated on his wrist. "His pulse is weak." Slowly she drew one finger over the inside of his wrist, searching back and forth, until she found the spot she was looking for. She pressed hard for several seconds. Lianco's deathly pale skin flushed red for about three seconds, and then faded again.

"What the hell was that?!" Violet demanded from beside Ariana.

But Ariana didn't move, or even turn at Violet's outburst. She kept her gaze on Lianco, searching for any sign that her treatment had worked. "It's something he taught me to do if one of us ever got hurt when he wasn't around. It will keep his blood circulating through his body for the next three minutes in case his heart fails. It will take us at least that long to get him to the Leku."

Ariana put an arm under Lianco's shoulders in an attempt to get him to a standing position. She struggled and I moved forward to help.

"I've got him. I need you to stay focused in case something unexpected happens. Violet can help me carry him."

Both of us looked to the left, where Violet had just been standing. Now she was gone. I searched for traces of her using my Roku skills, but I couldn't feel or recognize any of her usual movements or sounds. Violet was gone, and we had less than three precious minutes to get Lianco back.

*   *   *

With Ariana cradling his head and shoulders and me holding the rest of him, we raced Lianco along the passageways to the sterile rooms of the Leku. My highly sensitive eyesight acutely felt the impact of the change in light from outside the Realm to within. For me, the changes were drastic, from the yellow sunlight of the outside world to the welcome dark of the Realm, then to the brightly lit Leku sector. The effects were almost enough to make me decide to spend all my time either in or out. Ariana, I noticed, was feeling the change too.

We burst into the blindingly white main healing room. A bunch of startled young Lekus stared at our color-drained faces, and then at the limp figure we were carrying.

"Laic," I wheezed, "we need your help."

The thin man moved through his students, instructing

us to lay our baggage on a nearby table. Once we had laid Lianco down on the table, Laic chuckled.

"He's gotten himself hurt again, has he?"

Ariana rolled her eyes. "He's your brother, be serious. I performed the *cruentus* technique on him but it's been more than three minutes and I'm sure he's running out of oxygen." She was breathless with worry and urgency, but Laic was moving slowly to begin any treatment. It was all I could do not to smile. Had Lianco's injury been serious, I knew Laic would have already begun fixing him.

"The *cruentus* technique?" Laic laughed. "That's a clever move. Did this idiot teach you that?" He gestured to his brother's still, motionless form.

"Yes! Yes, of course! But why aren't you helping him?"

"Because he doesn't need it," Laic said calmly.

I had known Laic as long as I had known Lianco, as the two brothers were not far apart in age. They shared the same white-blond hair, but Laic's was wavy and full in comparison to Lianco's straight locks. They shared similar facial features, the only differences being a longer nose here, smaller ears there, and so on. But while their looks were the similar, their personalities were completely opposite. Laic was perpetually calm; nothing phased him. I had never seen Laic upset, though I had seen an enraged Lianco on more than one occasion. Laic was also a very talented Leku. His healing skills were excellent, almost as good as his brother's. Laic could have easily been chosen as the Council member for the Leku sector, which was the highest honor one could have in any sector. But Laic did not care whether or not he was selected for the

Council. He held a complete indifference to any position of power, and since Lianco had practically campaigned for the title, he had been chosen.

Though they were close, there had never really been any competition between them. Perhaps that was due to their opposite natures. If Laic and Lianco's personalities had matched, chaos might have ensued. But gentle Laic did everything in his power to avoid conflict, partly because Lianco was his elder brother, but mostly because he disliked confrontation of any kind. Laic hated yelling more than anything, claiming it upset his center of calm and disturbed his ability to heal.

So, I was surprised to see a small vein throbbing in Laic's head as the normally docile Ariana repeatedly shouted at him to do something. He was struggling to retain his composure.

"Ariana," I said quietly. She turned to look back at me with desperation in her eyes. "Let him do his job."

She sighed and put her hands over her face. I looked over her head at Laic, my eyes signaling him to continue.

"A man of few words, as usual, Darien," Laic chuckled as he ran both of his hands over each other, instantly sterilizing them with a single, quiet word. "But, I suspect you are also a man of many thoughts."

Laic navigated surely and swiftly over his brother's limp body, checking pressure points and pulse, and a hundred other things I could not begin to name. His students watched closely from across the room. Their eyes followed his every movement with intense concentration, and their faces reflected their admiration at his speed and ability.

Laic moved to a nearby counter, sifting through several boxes before making his way back to Lianco. He put two fingers under Lianco's nose and snapped, then pressed both fingers against his nostrils and covered his mouth to prevent any air from escaping. I could have sworn I saw a puff of white appear when Laic snapped, but in the blindingly white surroundings, even I couldn't be sure. Three seconds passed, then five, then ten. I could see the students looking at each other, their foreheads creased in doubt. Twenty-one seconds passed before Lianco jerked his brother's hands away and gasped for air.

"Am I in the sterile rooms?" Lianco muttered, barely able to form the words.

"Of course. I'll cover your eyes as you adjust." Laic placed a hand over Lianco's forehead, shielding his eyes from the blinding brightness. Lianco opened one eye slowly, then both dark blue irises came into view as he fought his way back to full consciousness.

"That was awful," he complained.

"What was?" Laic asked serenely.

"I just had a conversation with Serenu," Lianco stated flatly. Laic's face changed in an instant with this news. He was obviously shocked to hear that name.

Ariana turned to me, as though asking permission for something. I shrugged in response. She turned back toward the brothers, mouth already opened to ask her question.

"Does—" she began, but was cut off by Laic's outburst.

"Who does that bastard son think he is, and what is he doing *here?*" Laic said angrily.

Thirty-One

Liz

I could feel strong arms around me, protective arms, familiar arms. Still dazed, I couldn't bring myself to open my eyes. But Dan felt me stir.

"Liz?" he murmured in my ear. As I came to, I became aware that I was leaning against him. I felt his arm around my shoulders, and my head was slumped against his muscular chest. In the background, I could hear a faint hum that might have been the TV, but I still could not open my eyes.

"Or maybe, Zaria?" he whispered again, and then snickered.

"Shut up, you idiot," I said softly.

"Ah, so you are awake."

I decided right then that he officially knew me too well. Way too well, even for twins.

*   *   *

"Mom, I'm fine," I said into the receiver. "It was just some kind of a fainting spell. I feel better now, I just wanted to talk to you."

"Are you sure, honey?" My mother's concerned but shrill voice sounded in my ear. Her voice always got higher when she was nervous. "Because if you're not, your father and I can drive up there right now and bring you home."

"Really, mom, I'm totally fine. I just wanted to see how everything was in Brookwood."

I could hear my father talking to her, undoubtedly trying to take the phone out of her hands so he could get a few words in. That made me smile. A shushing sound from her and a few more rustles were heard before she spoke again.

"Well, if you're sure," she sounded reluctant. "Are you eating right? You know your body needs a lot of fuel with how skinny you are. If I know you, you're getting caught up in studying and reading, and missing meals. Do you need me to send you something? Some power bars or some of my award-winning bran muffins?"

I laughed. I could just picture my mom standing in the kitchen, flinging things left and right, looking for her brown sugar, just in case I said yes.

"I'm sure, mom. I'll talk to you guys later. Say hi to dad for me."

"Okay, sweetie. You take care of yourself!" she chirped into the phone before I hung up.

"Everything good with mom and dad?" Dan asked as he tossed me a bagel from the kitchen and sauntered toward my spot on the couch.

I popped a piece of the bagel into my mouth as the door to the apartment flew open. Alita and Orion instantly stood directly in front of me, and Dan dropped down behind the couch out of sight in case the new arrivals weren't friendly. I couldn't see the newcomers behind the human wall in front of me, but I heard a feathery, familiar voice. I craned my neck around them to see and caught a glimpse of silvery hair.

"Ariana!" I cried, throwing my legs out from the layers of pillows and blankets I had created and dashed toward her. My foot caught the end of one of the blankets, which would have sent me flying, but Ariana's petite, strong body caught me easily.

"Careful," she laughed. I heard Alita snort in the background but I didn't acknowledge it. I glanced up to see more people had entered the apartment. Both Darien and Lianco were here, as well as a new person I didn't recognize. Lianco saw my curiosity and quickly moved to introduce me to his brother. I figured there was some kind of relationship since they were practically mirror images of each other. Laic had different hair and was a little thinner than his brother, but Lianco had him in height. Lianco was at least two inches taller, maybe more.

"How did things go?" I overheard Orion ask Darien.

"Not here," he replied under his breath. I smiled at their abbreviated way of talking. The two of them had a serious lack of words.

Lianco either didn't hear them, or chose to ignore their exchange. "Well, we had an interesting experience out there, but that can wait for later. How did it go here? Is everyone safe?"

I had just sat back down on the sofa when Orion replied, "Yeah, we're all safe, but the princess over here fainted again." I threw him a nasty look in response, as did Alita.

"Well, I had good reason to faint. When I got out of the shower, there was writing on the wall in the bathroom," I explained. "Words written in blood."

I saw one eyebrow rise up in amusement on Laic's concerned face. I centered my emotions as I had taught myself to do and braced myself for their reactions. Laic watched me curiously, as if I was a specimen to be examined. Like I was a goldfish in a bowl.

"...not a big deal. It's about the third time she's..." Orion muttered through the side of his mouth. I had observed that Orion rarely spoke without unloading a great deal of sarcasm or without making a snooty comment. He was like a high school girl in that way.

"Put yourself in my place. You'd be traumatized too if all this was happening to you!" I snapped at him. Dan reappeared from behind the couch and, as he came closer, he placed a warning hand on my shoulder.

"Well, at least we know someone is back to normal," Dan joked.

"I know I haven't been acting like myself," I said sheepishly.

"Got that right," Dan said as he sat down beside me.

I smiled at his usual playfulness, but I could sense a strong undercurrent of unrest and irritability. All these days without any football or basketball practices to work off his energy must be tough for him, on top of all this weird stuff. We looked up to see the group around us had moved on in conversation, and we realized we were in our own little conversation bubble.

"Dan, we need to get outside," I whispered. "You need to play some ball. I can feel your hand twitching." He grimaced and nodded. "And I need to breathe some fresh air from the normal world and try to figure out what all this means."

"How can we get out?" he whispered back.

"No idea…"

I heard a faint voice in my head, calling my name. I looked around, confused as to the source, and finally raised my eyes toward Lianco, who was waving his hand near my face.

"Anyone home?" he inquired.

"Oh!" my cheeks flushed in embarrassment. "Sorry."

"We were discussing the situation at hand, and we have decided that your training must take place immediately."

"Training?" I echoed.

"As the Legends," he replied matter-of-factly.

"What kind of training?" I could hear the excitement in Dan's voice, as he realized that there was probably exercise involved in said training.

"The ancient training of the Alliance. Each of you must be trained in the abilities of all four sectors. The Rokenan possessed the abilities of Roku, Seiku, Leku, and Neku. They were born with these abilities and trained to know each of their skills, just as you will be." He looked me directly in the eyes. "You two are the last of the Rokenan."

Thirty-Two

Lianco

My brain was working as fast as it could. If Serenu truly knew where Loki was in the Unknown, assuming Loki was even alive, the world as we knew it was in danger. Loki's father had been an Original, and no doubt Loki had been trained for the position as well. If he gained access to the Book, life as we know it could be rewritten, and it was very possible the Realm could be lost forever.

It struck me as an odd twist of fate that we were placing all our faith, all our strength, and all our hope for the future in two college kids who had no Alliance training whatsoever. And to add to the already huge dilemma, these two were destined to be Rokenan, masters of all four sectors. They had demonstrated they had the guts, and maybe even the stamina, to be trained, but I was not sure that was going to be enough. Members of the Alliance generally began their training at three years of age, and do not become masters of a sector until age eighteen. Even then, the training continues as we are constantly enhancing our skills. It took me 190 years to become the Council Member for the Leku, the highest rank in my sector, and ten more years to become head of the Alliance, a position I have held for ten years and counting. I had invested 210 years to reach my highest capacity. Dan and Liz somehow needed to reach this level in one week, at the most.

We knew that we were strapped for time unlike any other point in our existence. The Council of Elders had already agreed to help with the training, but since they were still responsible for their sectors, their instruction alone might not be enough to help Dan and Liz succeed.

Alita, I sent at her. Her head didn't move but I knew I had her attention. *Do you think you and Orion could help your master with instruction?* One slow but sure nod answered my question. *I would ask Violet, but seeing as how she is gone...*

Eyes like fire turned in my direction. Crackles of blue sparks jumped from Alita's fingertips. *So I'm just second best?* she shot back. One small request had pushed her to where she was practically seething with anger. Perhaps it was the mention of Violet. Ariana sensed the tension and looked at me anxiously.

You're not second best, I answered. *I truly need your help.* But I got nothing in reply.

"We have to start your training immediately," I announced. Liz and Dan fixed their innocent gazes upon me. I knew they did not yet fully comprehend the pressure of the situation, telling them would only interfere with their focus.

"You haven't told us exactly what training entails," Liz stated.

"Darien and I will be helping with your Roku training," Ariana interjected. "I can only assume Lianco and Laic will teach you Leku." She looked in my direction for confirmation and I nodded my assent.

"Orion and I will be helping with your Seiku skills," Alita declared grudgingly. Orion whirled around, obviously surprised at being included as an instructor.

"We will?" he asked Alita.

"Yes, you will," I replied. "Alita will also help Guana teach you Neku, as she has a bit of experience in it herself."

Liz brightened a bit at the list of tutors she would have in this mysterious training. I knew she was very fond of Ariana and her relationship with Alita was pretty solid, thanks to the last few days. Dan seemed enthusiastic as well, though I could not imagine why. I had assumed he would be the more grudging participant.

"You start training in the morning," I said over my shoulder as Laic and I walked toward the door.

"Good luck!" Laic called just before the door thudded shut. Then he cut his eyes over to me and said, "They're truly going to need it."

Thirty-Three

Dan

I tried in vain to rub the sleep from my eyes as Liz and I were led down passageway after passageway by Ariana and Darien. There was no sunlight to judge by, but I could swear it was still the middle of the night.

"You will absolutely adore Master Skren," Ariana was telling Liz, who grinned from ear to ear with anticipation.

"I'm looking forward to it," she replied.

"At least someone's excited…" I mumbled under my breath. Liz looked over at me quizzically, and I sighed at having to explain my sarcasm.

"It's too early in the morning to be excited about anything, much less training," I explained. Liz punched me in the arm lightly.

"C'mon, be nice," she scolded, "this is exciting."

We made a sharp left turn and descended down yet another flight of stairs. I was getting tired of all the maze-like turns back and forth. Why couldn't these people make some gentle curves? Or better yet, live in regular buildings where daylight can be seen. Finally, we approached a set of ornate, antique doors.

"What is with the medieval theme?" I muttered. Darien turned around with such a look on his face that my eyes went wide and I readied myself for a punch from him.

"All of the sectors were built by the Originals, and the insides have been updated by each new Council. The outer parts of every sector were kept to their original designs, meaning they haven't been updated since the Middle Ages, around the year 417 A.D. The Council in place at the time thought it appropriate to keep the rugged, castle-like look for all future generations to see. You should respect their decisions, not question them."

My mouth fell open in a surprised O, and I stopped, pretty much frozen in my tracks. Darien turned away and pushed through the double doors. What they hadn't updated on the outside was compensated for on the interior.

The Roku training hall was like a complex workout facility mixed with a karate dojo. It had four floors, at least that I could see, all open to the front and wallpapered with mirrors. It was pretty obvious they had some of the most technologically advanced training equipment available. Treadmills, with response indication screens surrounding them to monitor progress, speed, and efficiency, lined the walls on one level. On another I could see the floor was covered with mats, and what looked like a karate class was practicing on them. On the third floor, in addition to the free weights and machines, I was surprised to see a multitude of weapons of all shapes and sizes lining one wall. On the other side, rows of dummies were available for target practice. Obviously, whoever the Master was, he didn't mind if his students practiced with everything from machetes to spears, shotguns, and daggers.

As we stood there looking, a sudden loud shout rang out

from the members of the 'karate' class. A figure descended a set of spiral stairs connecting the floors and approached us. He had only sweatpants on and his well-built shoulders and chest glistened with sweat. The pants were cropped just below his knees, and made of some kind of a cargo material, so I wasn't sure they even qualified as sweatpants.

As he approached, Ariana and Darien both snapped to attention. They were straight-backed so fast they almost created a breeze.

"Ariana, Darien," the man said with great pride in his voice.

"Master," they echoed.

"Ah," he said, noticing Liz and I, "you must be my new trainees."

"Yes. I mean yes, sir," Liz replied eagerly. "I mean, um, master."

"Master it is," he laughed. "Master Skren." I hadn't responded because I was examining him closely. The guy was either bald or had intentionally shaved his head, but either way I could practically see my reflection in his shiny skull. He wasn't particularly tall, maybe 5'7", but he was built like a brick wall with more muscle showing than I could ever hope to have.

"And your names?" he asked.

"I'm Dan, and she's Liz," I responded automatically. Master Skren raised one eyebrow.

"Your true names," Ariana whispered out of the corner of her mouth.

"Oh…" I was at a loss for words.

"I'm Zaria, and this is Zoran," Liz finished for me.

"Ah! Fine names!" the Master cried. "Zaria and Zoran; the Book chose well. Shall we?" He gestured back toward the stairs he had just descended.

We climbed the precarious metal steps with caution; there were no railings, but the Master and his experienced students all bounded up and down them with ease. As we walked onto the mats, I noticed a few lingering students surreptitiously watching us with open curiosity, and whispering among themselves. Master Skren turned to face Liz and me with Ariana and Darien at his sides.

"Well then, Zoran," he said casually, "why don't you throw a right jab at me?"

"What?" I asked.

"Throw a right jab."

"At you?"

"Yes," he chuckled. I looked at his set of muscles that made my well-defined shoulders look like a seventh grader's. I didn't want to punch him—he might retaliate, and I might regret it.

"Now?" I gulped, stalling as long as possible.

"Yes. Now."

The tone of his voice told me it was time to act, so I mustered all my strength and courage and threw my right arm toward his face as hard as I could. I'm not sure what happened next, but when I opened my eyes, I was staring up at the ceiling. My back ached and everyone was looking down at me.

"It looks like we have a lot of work to do," Master Skren

said with a smile. I groaned in response and tried to will myself to get up. Liz could hardly contain her laughter.

"What is so funny?" I hissed as I forced myself into a sitting position.

"That was incredible!" she laughed. "When you threw your jab, he moved an inch out of the way of your hand, then somehow got a hold of your ankle, and sent you flying! It was great!"

"Well," I said icily, "I'm glad you enjoyed the show. Let's see you try, *Zaria*." Her smile disappeared.

"Fine."

Everyone moved back into position on the mats, and Master Skren turned to Liz.

"Are you ready?"

Liz was visibly nervous, but she replied with a determined "yes" anyway. The Master instructed her to aim a strong right kick into his side. She positioned herself and forcefully swung her right leg around toward him the way she would kick a soccer ball into the goal. Her foot connected with his side with a loud thud. Liz was just as surprised as I was. After the last demonstration, neither of us expected her foot to make contact. But the Master hadn't budged. Not one inch of movement with that hard a kick.

"Not bad," Master Skren chuckled.

"But you let her hit you!" I protested.

"Yes," he said simply.

"Why?"

"Because I wanted to see how strong she was."

"But you didn't let me hit you…"

"Do you think I want a black eye?" he laughed. "I can see that you are strong, but your balance was so obviously off that I couldn't resist turning your attack against you."

He laughed boisterously, and even Darien and Ariana smiled. Then Master Skren focused his attention back to Liz.

"Have you played soccer?" he asked.

"Yes."

"I can tell. Your leg muscles are very strong."

Liz smiled, not only pleased by the compliment, but also relieved that she hadn't ended up flat on her back as I had.

"Now, Darien and Ariana will show you two where to change. Then maybe football boy here can redeem himself."

My mouth gaped open as Darien dragged me away. I had never told him I played football, so how did he know?

"He's quite observant," Darien said, reading my face and interpreting my thoughts. "That is something you will learn as well."

*   *   *

When we regrouped on the mats, Liz and I looked like something out of an action movie. The tan colored shirt I was wearing was made of a soft, breathable material that I don't think qualified as cotton. I had on a pair of cut off cargo-like pants, similar to the Master's. Liz was in the female version of the uniform, I suppose. She appeared in a form fitting white shirt made of the same material as mine, with tight, stretchy brown leggings. Her curly hair was pulled back into a sleek french braid, which I had to assume was the handiwork of Ariana, since I had never seen her wear it that way before. Darien and Ariana had also changed their clothes and were dressed identically to us, except Ariana's silver hair was pulled into a long ponytail that hung down her back.

Liz and I faced Master Skren, prepared for our next challenge, but extremely nervous about what might be in store for us.

"What kind of material is this?" I whispered to Liz as the Master and Ariana talked quietly together.

"No idea," she whispered back. "Feels like a silky cotton, but it molds to my skin more like spandex." She pointed to her own tight shirt and demonstrated what she meant. With just a little tug, the shirt didn't move at all. She had to really pull to get it to budge.

"Whatever it is, it's very comfortable," she whispered. "But these leggings are weirding me out."

"Leggings? Is that what you call those?" I asked casually, trying to save my manhood since I had already identified them as such.

"Yeah," she replied. "I don't dislike them, it's just that I would normally wear something over them, so I feel kind of naked."

"Well then, trainees," Master Skren interrupted, "if you two are finished chatting, we will get started." The smile disappeared from his face. "Welcome to my version of hell."

Liz

We spent the rest of the day cramming years worth of training into a few hours. Dan and I practiced speed, agility, and fighting techniques. We learned how to correctly handle and fight with long swords, spears, daggers, machetes, and almost every other weapon imaginable. We trained on accuracy with guns, and learned the art of hand to hand combat. We were physically worn out, and our brains were fried from taking in so much new information. But, we seemed to be succeeding in learning since Ariana and Darien were pleased with our progress.

I learned that the shirts and pants we were wearing were made of a substance called nanocloth, a protective material which had a strength equivalent to two sets of body armor. Not only did this clothing protect the body during combat situations, it also protected us against equally destructive magic attacks. I was especially glad to have such protection when we stopped practicing with dummies and began battling each other.

Without warning, Ariana hefted a long sword and flew at me with lightning speed, and I barely had enough time to parry the blow. Out of the corner of my eye, I could see Darien zooming toward Dan with two short daggers and a flurry of martial arts-like motion. His speed was mesmerizing. Unfortunately, I had little time to watch because my opponent wasn't backing off.

Ariana struck again and again, each blow more forceful than the last. Quite a few strikes snuck past my blade at first, and, as predicted, the nanocloth protected me from injury. As the sparring continued, the number of blows that she was able to get past my defenses became fewer and fewer, until I realized I was gaining the skill to block her attacks every time. Soon I began to take the upper hand, sneaking some pretty impressive strikes past her blade, my longsword grazing or even hitting her arm but not leaving a mark. My newfound success clearly surprised her. Ariana's eyes narrowed with intensity as she realized she had transitioned from teacher to legitimate opponent. I let out a triumphant yell as I forced her backward. I couldn't see how Dan was doing, but if the grunts coming from his direction were any indication, his battle with Darien had taken the same turn as mine.

After 10 minutes of intense, continuous fighting, Master Skren raised his hands and instructed us to stop.

"Well," he said, after giving everyone a moment to catch their breath, "I am certainly impressed." His eyes skimmed across our tired, panting forms, and he smiled knowingly. "There's no doubt that you have Roku abilities, my friends."

"Thank you," Dan and I managed to pant.

"You have done well to learn the art of battle, and you are learning to use your abilities to anticipate attacks and counter blows. You still have one major Roku lesson left to learn: the power of the senses. To truly conquer an enemy, you must be able to call on your sight, smell, touch, and hearing to aid you. It is not enough to just fight the battle at hand. You must also be able to instantly gather and assess information about what has happened previously, what is happening in the present moment, and what may happen in the future in any given situation."

Dan and I nodded as if we understood, but deep down inside I was unsure about what Skren's lesson might entail. We used our senses every day, but it was unclear how we could use them to predict the future. It was one thing to learn to fight, but to become a mind reader?

"Sit down in a meditative position on the mat," Master Skren instructed. "Now close your eyes and clear your minds."

We sat down where we had been standing, crossing our legs over each other Indian style and resting our hands at our sides.

"I want you to focus on using your senses. Hear our footsteps, hear the sound of the blade cutting through the air. Feel the vibrations as we move around you. Smell the metal of the blade. And remember, keep your eyes closed and your mind focused. Do not fear; we will not hit you. For now, just take it all in."

I closed my eyes and let the darkness completely wash over me. I heard soft footsteps and felt a slight vibration to my left. Such dainty footsteps could only be Ariana's. Her weapon dance continued around us, and I heard her blade whistle past my ears on more than one occasion. Darien joined the circling next. He was identifiable by his slightly louder and heavier steps. He also had a recognizable breathing pattern that gave away his identity, which I was sure he would not want to hear about. His razor sharp daggers circled my head, their short blades whistling as they cut the air, and I did my best not to flinch at the deadly sounds. Master Skren was last. His footsteps were barely audible and he made no vibration that I could detect. The only thing I could tell was that he moved with blinding speed.

The weapon he carried was new to me. It made a deeper sound as it moved through the air, almost as if it was not willing to move as fast as he was making it. Whatever he carried was slammed into the ground next to me, and the hollow sound waves identified it as a staff. Finally, all movement ceased and silence took over. I slowly relaxed and sat quietly in the silence.

"Don't move," Master Skren warned. "We're going to go through the exercise again. But this time, watch your heads, because we will be going in for the kill."

I took a deep breath and I heard Dan do the same. I steadied myself and tried to focus on not being afraid. Darien was first this time. I heard his daggers coming the second they started spinning and slashing. Instinctively, my head ducked left and right, narrowly missing the whizzing blades that would have surely severed my nose or ears. Ariana harped on Dan, and though I could not see him, I could hear the air moving with his bobbing and weaving. He, too, was dodging the edge of her blade. Skren was last, as he had been before, but this time I didn't hear him coming. I *felt* him more than heard him, and ducked out of the way just in time. His staff barely grazed my right ear. He let out a surprised grunt, and then he was everywhere. His staff tried every angle surrounding my head and shoulders. He tested me to my limits. Then he moved toward Dan, while Darien and Ariana circled around me like hawks.

I thought the madness would go on forever, but finally Master Skren gave a curt command and the weapons were still. Dan and I opened our eyes and blinked rapidly at the brightness of the room. All three of our aggressors were standing in front of us, breathing hard. Darien looked annoyed, but Ariana wore a proud smile.

"Well, well, well," Master Skren smiled. "I did not think you would be able to withstand our attack. I thought it would be impossible for you to fend off all three of us at the same time with no training prior to today." He sighed deeply, put his hands together, and gave a slight bow. "You have proven me wrong. No one but a true Rokenan could master an entire sector's training in one day. Welcome, friends, as members of the Roku."

Ariana trotted over toward the wall of weapons and retrieved a tiny silver box from a hidden compartment in the wall itself. The Master took the delicate box in his rough hands and opened it to reveal a pool of ink. Into the ink he dipped one finger, and stepped toward me. Taking my wrist, he turned it over and pressed the tip of his finger to my skin. The spot burned for a moment, but when he lifted his finger, an intricate design remained. "That is the mark of the Roku," he explained. "If you ever need help, simply show this mark to another Roku. We are all one." He gave the same mark to Dan.

ROKU

147

Once I had recovered from the shock of getting my first tattoo, I raised my hand tentatively.

"This is not a classroom, Zaria," he laughed. "We are all friends here. If you have something to ask, please feel free to do so."

"Well," I began, "out of curiosity, why did you help us? I mean, from what I understand, the Rokenan were deliberately destroyed by the other sectors, so I thought you would hate us."

"Why would I hate someone I do not know?" he asked. I opened my mouth to speak but Master Skren beat me to it. "You ask me why I helped you? Because that is my duty. That is my responsibility. The Book endowed me this responsibility many years ago—back in my younger years as a Being."

"Does that mean you're old?" Dan interrupted.

"In human years, yes, but not in the years of Beings. I am only 312 years old."

Dan's jaw dropped and his eyes bugged out. I elbowed him in the side to remind him of his manners.

"Anyway," Master Skren continued, "Roku was not the sector that started the war. The Seikus let their envy overrule their good judgement. They convinced everyone else they were in the right and that all others should support them by joining their quest. That war was ages ago, and I was never a part of it. So, no, I have never held any resentment toward the Rokenan."

The ancient doors to the training facility creaked open and Lianco strode through. Ariana's eyes lit up and she happily waved at him, until she saw Alita slip through the door right behind him. Her face instantly fell, and she caught my gaze. She shrugged at my raised eyebrows and abruptly turned away.

Thirty-Five

Lianco

I saw Ariana wave and raised my hand to wave back, but she had already turned away. Alita swept past me and hurried up the stairs to Liz and Dan. With very few words, she ushered them back down to the main level and out the door.

"Where's she going in such a hurry?" Ariana asked critically as I climbed the last two steps.

"She is taking them back to the apartment," I replied. Her face darkened slightly.

"I thought that was my job," she said irritably.

"It was, but now you are needed elsewhere." I turned to face both her and Darien. "Violet is still missing. I need the two of you to scour the area to see if you can find her."

"What about the Unknown?" Darien asked carefully.

"There is no change in the layers...I have been watching closely."

Master Skren quietly excused himself, saying he had other students to attend to. Once he was gone, the two of them turned on me.

"What's the deal with Violet?"

"Where's the Book?"

"Do you think this is serious?"

"What's really going on?"

"Hold it!" I cried. "Too many questions. If you would

like an explanation, I will tell you what little I know. Serenu has the Book with him in the Unknown. Violet has gone to who knows where, and at best we have less than a week to get two complete amateurs fully trained for whatever is coming."

"He's in the Unknown? Are you sure?" Ariana asked softly. "But that's where—"

"Yes, that is where Loki disappeared to. Loki, the son of an Original. And, if Loki has somehow survived all these years, then he would still remember the secrets of the Book. He could rewrite the past and change the future. He could essentially destroy everyone in the Realm with a simple spell."

"Everyone?" Darien asked.

"Everyone…we are all in grave danger."

*   *   *

Liz and Dan were splayed out on the couch, engrossed by the television when I entered the apartment. Empty containers and greasy plates littered the kitchen countertop.

"What was for dinner?" I asked casually.

"Fried chicken!" Liz answered from the couch. "And it was unbelievably good!"

"Really? Fried chicken?"

"Yep! It's been so long since either of us have had good, southern, Tennessee-quality fried chicken."

"Maryland doesn't do fried chicken any justice," Dan agreed.

"But how…?" I wondered aloud.

"I used the portal to go to Tennessee," Alita whispered as she appeared out of the wall. A blue rectangle shimmered away behind her. She walked past me and handed Dan a small box with a thin silver handle. "There you go, the world's finest chow mein," she smiled. I rolled my eyes, knowing that letting her keep an ability like that would come back to haunt me.

"Did you get the Chinese food in Tennessee too?" I asked. She glanced at me with a sarcastic look, and then turned back to face the television. The room was silent, except for the obnoxious voice of some TV personality the three of them were watching.

What are you doing? I sent.

Making them happy, and being useful for once, she sent back.

You are useful all the time.

No, I'm not, and you know it.

I sighed and rubbed my temples. Sparring with Alita was difficult, and even more of a strain when we were communicating with *allreçu*.

"Well, regardless of your dinner choices, I came here to congratulate you two. You surprised everyone by completing the Roku training in a single day. And you definitely earned the respect of Master Skren, which is a difficult feat on its own."

"Thank you!" Liz sing-songed. She was happily munching on a drumstick and secretly eyeing the box of chow mein in Dan's hands.

"Tomorrow you hit the books in the Neku sector, so I

would advise you to put away all that greasy food, get away from the television, and get a good night's sleep," I warned. "Guana is not your average librarian."

Liz

I believe I have just died and gone to heaven, I thought to myself as we walked through the open doors. The entrance itself was huge, and the doors were significantly bigger than the ones leading into the room that contained the Book, or the ones we passed through to enter the Roku training area. These doors were at least 50 feet high, maybe more, and they appeared to be made of mahogany because they were a rich, dark maroon that shone in the light. Intricate patterns, similar to the new mark on my wrist, were carved into the doors, but what was behind them was even more fascinating.

The outer wall of the room was lined with thousands upon thousands of books in neat rows, resting on long shelves that ran down the full length of the room and all the way to the ceiling. Each wall had at least four rolling ladders, some longer than others, so even the highest books could be reached. The ceiling of the library was as tall as its doors, and the room must have been as long as a football field. The interior of the room itself was also surrounded by, and filled with, books. Shelves at least ten feet tall filled the room in neat rows parallel to the walls, creating the typical library maze. These shelves also had ladders for easy access to the top books. By the look of awe on his face, even Dan was impressed. Libraries had never been his thing, as they had been mine, but this one was more impressive than either of us had ever seen.

Through gaps in the shelves, I thought I could see little feet and arms, and I was pretty sure I heard the pitter-patter of feet scurrying back and forth. I was trying to make sense of it all, so I did not see the little creature that approached.

"Hello, Gomer!" Alita said from beside us.

I peered down at Gomer. He stood even with my thigh and had a bulbous body that was anything but human. He seemed to be made of some type of hard, dark green, almost black, material. It resembled rock, but was definitely not a geological substance I had ever seen before. Short, turtle-like arms and legs protruded from his round, rock-like center, and all four appendages ended in claws. As he turned slightly to greet Alita, I noticed a small tail. His head resembled that of a turtle's, but with a less pronounced jaw and a small nose. His beady, black eyes examined us with noticeable contempt.

"You are Zaria and Zoran, yes?" he asked. His voice was high-pitched, and he had a distinct British accent. Frankly, I wasn't expecting such an intelligent manner from such a strange-looking creature.

"Yeah," Dan replied.

"Yeah?" Gomer mimicked. "I expect 'yes' from such highly praised Beings." He snorted. "By the looks of it, you won't last one hour here."

"Gomer," Alita chided. "Be nice to them, they're new at this." Gomer rolled his beady little eyes.

"Um, I don't mean to be rude, but what kind of creature are you?" I asked. Gomer turned to glare at me.

"What am I?" he echoed snidely. "You silly, *silly* girl. It's not polite to ask such a question, but as Alita has cautioned me to be nice, I shall at least provide an answer. I am part of an ancient species of highly intellectual and witty beings known as the golems. We are reputed to have the best knowledge retention of any species ever found. We have at least three times the memory of elephants—we never forget anything."

Gomer looked imperious as he recited his credentials. It was a well-rehearsed speech; obviously he had to give it often. I had begun to feel a little sorry for him, so I reached out tentatively. I was totally unprepared for his outburst when he saw my fingernails.

"Dear heavens!" he cried. "You expect me to let *these* fingers touch my precious babies?"

"They're just a little dirty—"

"A little dirty? My word, they're filthy! *Look* at those nails. The paint is chipped and you have dirt all under there. And your cuticles! I don't suppose you've been training with Master Skren recently?"

"Yes," I replied sheepishly. "All day yesterday."

"Well, that will do it. All those weapons and not nearly enough sterilization. Tsk, tsk." I tried my best not to blush or laugh. "Gloria!" he yelled to a nearby golem. "I need a chair and my kit!"

Gloria must have heard the exchange and anticipated Gomer's request because she appeared almost immediately with a chair, a box, and two other golems. The two of them motioned for me to sit down. The chair could only be classified as a stool, but it put me at the right height for these small creatures. Gomer stepped up to my left, and Gloria followed suit on my right. The two other golems stood at the ready.

"File!" Gomer cried, holding out a sharp claw. I was surprised at the gentleness of his touch when he grabbed my wrist. With a flurry of claws, comments, and instruments, Gomer and Gloria filed, cleaned, shined, and clear coated my nails.

"Voila!" Gomer said with pride as he spread his mouth really wide into what I assumed was a smile. I stood up to say my thanks, but before I could speak, Alita grabbed Dan and pushed him down onto the vacated stool. Despite his protests, he received the same treatment, minus the clear coat. He was adamant about that. As soon as Gomer pulled out the polish, Dan started yelling until he put it back in the box.

A little blue winged thing dropped from the ceiling to hover beside Gomer and whisper something in his ear. Looking more closely, I could see it had a small blue head with a tiny hair protruding straight up from it. Little bat wings flapped furiously to hold up the small blue, human-like body. Tiny talons lined its front legs, which tapped together as it waited for a response from Gomer. Gomer whispered back into the hair on its blue head, which I guessed functioned as an ear. I saw another similar creature, hovering near the ceiling, zip out of sight as soon as Gomer finished speaking.

"Guana will see you now," Gomer announced primly. Noting my befuddled expression, he sighed. "That, my dear, was an imp. Fastest way to send information, you know.

Their brains are interconnected…it's a very fascinating science…"

I nodded. That explained why the first imp didn't move after Gomer whispered in its ear, but the second one did. I shook my head and laughed to myself at how rationally I was beginning to think about all these strange creatures and situations.

We followed Gomer through the huge room, weaving our way through the tall bookshelves to a door at the back of the library. The woman who waited for us inside looked ancient—older than old. She was quite small, her hair was pure white, and her face sagged all over. She looked like a sweet, old grandmother, with double the wrinkles.

"Hello, Guana," Alita said softly as we entered. The little woman looked up and smiled.

"Hello, dear one," Guana said. She, too, spoke softly, and with a British accent. "Have you brought the Legends with you?"

"Yes, they're here."

"Good, good."

She sprang up from behind her desk, surprisingly quick for an old woman, and immediately marched past us and out the door we had just entered. She wasn't a whole lot taller than the golems, but walked straight-backed and so swiftly, that we had to jog to catch up with her.

"Whoa, grandma's got a serious power walk," Dan muttered beside me.

"Goshen!" Guana barked. "I need every book we have on the Rokenan and each sector's Book. Now!"

*   *   *

Guana turned out to be the opposite of what she appeared. She was, in fact, a no-nonsense, bossy, nosy, action-oriented sector Master who was extremely intelligent; not anything like the homely little grandmother type she seemed at first. Guana was an amalgamation of all the great minds that ever lived. She explained that her photographic memory enabled her to remember literally everything she read. Therefore, she had a deep knowledge of mathematics, physics, geography, and classic literature. She knew the genus name for every species, as well as their specific characteristics, and she could recite obscure facts like the names of all known stars. The amount of information she knew was much more than one could fathom, and her recall was astonishing. Even more surprising was the fact that most of her golems knew almost as much as she did. And what they didn't know off the top of their crusty little heads, they could easily find among the stacks of books in the immense library.

According to Guana, we had approximately six hours to learn about our history as Rokenan, as well as learn the histories of the rest of the Alliance. Every sector. Every event. Word for word if we were able. I heard Dan sigh loudly as he flipped through the Book of Seiku. A few minutes passed, and he sighed again, louder this time. I looked up from the Book of Leku I was reading, but he didn't sense me staring. After the third sigh, I glared at him until he looked at me. He innocently shrugged. I rolled my eyes. He could be such a child sometimes. I focused my eyes back on the fascinating material in the Leku Book I was studying.

After about an hour of studying each sector, four straight hours in all, Guana laid another gigantic ancient book down on the table in front of us. Dust bloomed out of its yellowed pages and caused coughing fits among those of us seated there.

"What is that?" I managed to choke out in between coughs.

"This," Guana said proudly, "is the Book of Rokenan."

The Book of Rokenan was slightly smaller than the Books of the other sectors, but it looked twice as old. Dan groaned and reached over for it. He tried to open the cover but couldn't. It didn't even budge. He tried again and again, but nothing happened.

"The Book must be opened correctly. You haven't done that yet," Alita chuckled from behind us.

"So how do I open it correctly?" Dan asked mockingly. "Start at the back? Say the magic word?"

"You don't have to act smart, Dan."

Guana explained, "The Book was sealed after we found it so that its knowledge was not available to just anyone. There are secrets inside not all should be privy to. There are special words to open it, in fact. Simply repeat after me," she said. "*Clavis patofacto.*"

"*Clavis patofacto,*" Dan echoed.

"Good, now place your hand over the binding and say it."

Dan placed his hand over the binding and repeated the phrase. "*Clavis patofacto.*" There was a soft click and the cover opened with ease. The pages inside were just as dusty as the outer binding, but they were significantly yellowed and moldy. I reached out and touched the first page and the corner of it immediately disintegrated. From behind us, I saw Gomer's small form darting through the shelves toward us.

"Wait!" he cried. "Don't touch it! Your hands haven't been protected yet!"

"Protected?" I echoed.

Without a word, Gomer placed his hands on either side of mine. A weird, tingling feeling shot through my hands. When he took his hands away, mine were glowing slightly. Gomer did the same procedure with Dan, and I noticed that Dan's hands glowed slightly blue as opposed to my pale yellow. I looked over at Gomer for permission, and then reached out with a glowing finger to touch the first page again. I released my held breath when I saw that the page stayed intact. Together, the five of us focused on the words written there. It was a journal entry, or something like it, hastily written and stained with what could only be blood. The name scratched at the top of the page read 'Trian.' I assumed he was the author of the most recent entry. His words detailed the horrors—of the genocide, war, and betrayal of the Rokenan; his emotions poured out through his words. Toward the bottom of the page, he even foretold of our arrival. My hands were shaking as I traced his words. "Do not fear—the Legends will come."

"He knew about us," Dan whispered. "But how?"

Thirty-Seven

Dan

We spent the next few hours paging through our culture's original history, reading and learning about the Rokenan. There was so much to take in, more than I thought my brain could absorb. I knew Liz could get it, genius that she was. The pages in the book were packed with various works of literature. Narratives, journal entries, poems, and songs filled the bindings, cover to cover. All of them spoke of the history of the Rokenan…

We were yet another sector in the famed Alliance. Rokenan joined the Alliance around the same time Caesar Augustus ruled the Roman empire. We had emerged victorious from a war with the Seiku, who, though defeated, were also allowed to join the Alliance. Life seemed perfect. The Neku sector was in the process of drawing up plans for a common center for the Alliance, a place where all could exist together. In the meantime, the Rokenan were living in their homeland of Crete, a place they described as their personal paradise. Each sector lived somewhere in the world, though they were not really *of* the world. Apparently, the Rokenan had descended from the Romans, so we lived not far from our homeland.

Other sectors moved as far as halfway around the globe from their original heritage. Easily hidden, the Neku sector spread throughout Britannia, while the Leku hid themselves in the arctic chill of northern Asia, soon to be Russia. Their naturally pale skin tones blended well with the people of that area. The Seiku wandered on their own through what would later come to be known as Greenland. The Roku sector took pride in their strength and hid themselves in the plains of Africa, isolated from other native civilizations amongst the lions and elephants. They stayed in Africa until the civil wars began. Over time, their tanned skin paled out once more as they moved north and eventually hid themselves with the Neku in Brittania during the wars.

The sectors were friendly, or so everyone thought. At some point, however, the Seikus became jealous. As users and protectors of the elements, they had strong emotions, and the famed battle between a Seiku and a Rokenan was the last straw. Jealousy and rage overtook them and a power struggle ensued. One by one, the sectors joined the resistance until there was no more hope for the Rokenan...

Liz leaned back in her chair and stretched her neck side to side. I closed the cover of the Book and sighed. Blood, death, war, pain; why did it always come to that? For the Alliance, it meant disrupting each of the sectors and driving them out of their respective paradises. Throwing "us," I suppose I should have said, since Liz and I were now smack dab in the middle of it.

After a few minutes, Guana once again appeared in front of the table with Alita at her side. The two of them proceeded to quiz us on what we had learned. Liz and I fired responses back with surprising ease, confident in our answers, and astounded at the depth of our knowledge. We were both surprised at how much I, specifically, had been able to absorb in such a short time. At last, our teachers were satisfied. Alita smiled in approval and Guana gave a toothless grin.

"You are ready," she said.

Gomer appeared beside her with a small, bronze box clutched in his claws. Guana opened the box and instructed us to hold out our wrists. The burning sensation returned as the ink on her finger dug itself into our skin. When she finally took her finger away, another design was left in its place, representing the completion of our Neku training.

NEKU

"Thank you, Guana," Liz said as she examined the marking.

"It is my pleasure, child," Guana replied. "You have earned it."

Thirty-Eight

Lianco

I paced nervously back and forth in my office. There were two more sectors to train with and only four days remaining. Things had gone well so far, but could it last? I suspected that Liz and Dan's biggest challenge was going to be Seiku. Master Kailen hated the Rokenan with a passion, and he had always trained his students to feel the same way.

In my anxious state I did not notice Ariana enter the room. She simply watched and waited. When I finally saw her, she was curled up in one of the armchairs, her eyes closed peacefully. Her silver hair was strewn across the arm of the chair and partially covered her face. I reached out tentatively and touched a silver wisp.

"I was wondering how long it would take you to notice me," she murmured with her eyes still closed. "Are you worried?"

"Yes…very much," I replied. "If this does not go right, if something happens to either of them, I—"

"You'll be fine," she interrupted. "We all will." She unfolded her tangled limbs and cupped a hand against my face. Her hands were always warm, so I was more than willing to let my head droop against her open palm. She motioned for me to sit down, and I did, with my back against her chair. Her hands began combing through my hair, gently erasing every knot and tangle. As her nails dragged lightly across my scalp, I felt a series of tantalizing shivers shoot down my spine. Involuntarily, my head tilted back into her lap. Her beautiful, gray eyes smiled back at me.

"I miss the green," I whispered. Her smile faded.

"Well, you have your brother to thank for that," she said sadly.

"Yet another reason to kill him."

Her eyes danced once more. I smiled and closed my own, waiting for the thrill of her fingers to resume. I was surprised instead when I felt warmth on my lips and hair tickling my ears. I opened my eyes and came face to face with Ariana's chin. I was surprised, not sure how to react. She noticed my discomfort and pulled away, looking deeply into my eyes once more.

"Sorry," she murmured. Without a word, I turned around, and took her face in both of my hands.

"No apology necessary," I whispered against her lips. We had not been alone in quite some time, and I moved as slowly as I could despite my eagerness. She must have felt similarly, for both hands snaked around my neck and embedded themselves in my hair, securing my face to hers. I wrapped my arms around her waist as she knelt in the chair, our lips and hearts moving faster and faster.

"Lianco, I—" The door had swung open and there stood Alita, dumbstruck. Pure guilt showed on every inch of my face. Ariana's hands were still tangled in my hair and her eyes were hard as rocks.

"Do you need something?" she asked icily.

"Yeah, I need you to leave so I can talk to Lianco," Alita snapped.

"That's not going to happen," Ariana said flatly.

"Aw, did I interrupt the best day of your life?" Alita sneered.

"Yes, you did."

"Sorry," Alita rolled her eyes. "I didn't know you Rokus were such backstabbers."

"And I didn't know all Seikus were whores," Ariana said, returning fire.

Alita's jaw dropped to the floor, but that did not stop Ariana from continuing her acid words.

"First Serenu, and now you want Lianco? Talk about sibling rivalry…"

"I do not want—"

"You do and you know it. Everyone knows it by how blatantly it's written on your face. How sweetly you talk to him. How you're always helpful. Blah, blah, blah…"

"You just have something against me because of what Serenu did to you," Alita said quietly. Her voice was full of emotion.

"Oh! You mean the way he *ruined* me?" I had never seen Ariana so angry. She stood up and walked over to the door. "Yes, ruined. Do you think I wanted this hair and these eyes? Has it never occurred to you that I liked being myself? Now I'm some washed out version of my former self with a big scar and terrible nightmares. So you listen closely, Alita. When, and if, Serenu shows himself, I'm going to kill him. By whatever means necessary. And you will never, ever, get Lianco."

Alita stood open mouthed as her eyes filled with tears. She stormed away and Ariana sagged; her unusual outburst had drained her strength. Darien swept into the room moments later. We stared at each other for a few seconds before I was able to speak.

"Can I help you?" I asked quietly.

"Um, I came to get your feedback on our results from the search," he replied.

"The search for Violet?"

"Yes."

"How did that go?" I asked. Darien looked puzzled. Then he turned to Ariana.

"You haven't told him?"

"No." She smiled sheepishly. "I hadn't gotten to that yet."

"Well, then," Darien said, "the search itself was unsuccessful. Or perhaps it was successful, depending on how you look at it. We found nothing. A few bits of magical residue here and there, but nothing worth following. We scoured the area in a 50 mile radius, but Violet appears to be gone."

"Gone," I repeated dumbly.

"Yes, gone."

"Our secret weapon is gone."

"I thought Zoran and Zaria were our secret weapons," Darien said with a quizzical look.

"But if they fail—"

"Oh, no, let's not get started on that again," Ariana interjected. "They're going to be ready. You need to believe that. We are not in a crisis yet, Lianco. Relax."

I took a deep breath and let her words wash over me. Relax. I could do that. Or, at least I hoped I could.

Thirty-Nine

Liz

I heard footsteps approaching, clomping down the hallway, from at least one hundred feet away before the door swung open. Dan and I were practicing our Roku concentration, but both of us were startled out of our reveries when Alita walked in. I guess we had not yet memorized the pattern of her steps.

Alita herself was a sight. Her usually neat hair was practically standing on end, creating a halo of black strands around her head. Her face was blotchy and tear-stained. I got up to go to her but she stopped me mid-stride.

"Don't come near me. You can't touch me," she said with one hand out to signal me to stop.

"Um, why not?" I asked.

"Because I'm upset, and that makes me dangerous."

"I can see you've been crying. That's why I want to help."

"But you can't because I'm upset inside. I got mad and tried to take a wall out with electricity. My tears short-circuited my magic and now all of it is stuck inside me," she said.

"What can I do? Call somebody? Get help?"

"Go get a towel; make sure it's absolutely dry. And, I'm going to need a metal ballpoint pen."

I ran to get a towel and Dan went looking for a pen. As I approached Alita, she cautioned me again not to touch her or else I would absorb the shock. I gently tossed her the towel and she wiped off her tear-stained face. Dan came back with a pen.

"Dan, I need you to take the ink out of the pen," she instructed. Dan did as he was told without bothering to ask why. "Okay, now put it on the floor." He did. Then Alita turned to us.

"Both of you need to stand back," she said, wincing, "and you might want to cover your eyes." We watched from a distance as her mouth moved very quickly and then she touched the pen. Upon contact, the room exploded with a bright white light. There was a loud crack that transformed into a resounding boom, followed by a strong whoosh of air, and then it was over. Dan and I had to blink a few times to clear the aftereffects of the blinding light.

Alita was sitting on the ground, eyes blank and staring. She had a gash about two centimeters from her right eye, and another on the hand she had used to touch the pen. That gash started at the knuckle of her index finger and went all the way back to the middle of her forearm. Dozens of other tiny scratches covered her arms and face, as did black soot.

"Oh my god!" I cried, as I rushed to her side. Tears sprang to my eyes at the thought of her being truly wounded.

"We have to get her to Leku," Dan said. "Do you remember the way?" I nodded, glad that for once Dan was in charge and he was making the decisions. He lifted her up in both arms like a princess, and her head bounced against his shoulder as we ran toward help.

*   *   *

I couldn't watch as Laic cleaned the wounds, preparing them to be healed. The biggest problems were those two gashes, but everything else had been healed immediately with no prep necessary.

"So," Laic asked, "what exactly happened?" From the expression on his face I couldn't tell whether he was concerned or amused by the whole ordeal. Weirdly, that gave me some comfort, since he wouldn't be so light-hearted if Alita was badly hurt.

"She came in all…electric, and then she touched a pen and the whole room exploded," Dan exclaimed. Of course, Dan's anxiousness was causing him to leave out a few details.

I sighed and tried to fill in the gaps. "She came in crying with her hair sticking out all over the place, and told us she was 'upset inside.' We took the ink out of a pen and gave it to her, and when she touched it, whatever was upset inside her exploded the pen and created this mess." I gestured to her face.

"Crying?" Laic mused. "Ah, then she must have been angry with Lianco."

"What?" I asked. "Why?

"Well, because he and Ariana…"

My eyebrows shot up. "He and Ariana what?"

"You haven't noticed?" Dan looked shocked. "I thought it was obvious they had a thing going."

I couldn't have been more surprised, and my brother's casual observation aggravated me. Of course, Dan would notice. Ever the ladies' man, he was tuned in to body language signals and he would have naturally picked up on hers.

"Lianco and Ariana have had a 'thing' for a very long time," Laic explained. "It started just after our qualifying tests and has been going on ever since. They try to keep it hidden, but sometimes Ariana goes to his office for solace, especially given what happened to her." Laic's bemused expression turned dark, and I heard him mutter something about a son of some sort.

"Okay...what is this thing that happened to Ariana that everyone keeps mentioning?" I asked, a little hurt that I had not already been told.

"Although I think Ariana should tell you herself, considering how close you've become in such a short time, I suppose it's only fair that you know," Laic said. He stole a glance at Alita, who still appeared unresponsive in her spaced out state.

"Do you know who Serenu is?" he asked. Dan and I nodded.

"Well, Ariana and Serenu trained as Roku together. They were very close friends who shared just about everything, except Lianco. Ariana had also grown close to Lianco. Although she was not with him yet, they were very good friends.

Ariana became the unofficial mediator of the hostility between the two brothers. She was always trying to diffuse tension or break up a fight between them. They rarely talked to each other, but each would confide in her. Serenu was glad to have Ariana as his friend, proud that he got to spend more time with her because they were in the same sector. Lianco's training kept him in the Leku sector, and Serenu gloated over the fact that he had closer proximity to Ariana. Serenu thought he had it all, but a darkness was brewing in him that was generations old.

"Ariana wasn't aware that Serenu secretly practiced Seiku magic after their scheduled training sessions and late at night. He wanted to be dually gifted, like Lianco, so he practiced some of the traditional magic and some that he actually created himself. What he did not realize at the time was any new magic not put in the Seiku spell book is a recipe for disaster.

"When Serenu took his qualifying tests, he was the only Roku trainee who didn't pass. Somehow his secret magic interfered with his Roku skills. When he realized he had made a huge mistake, he was furious. He stormed out of the testing area and into the arms room. Like a true friend, Ariana went after him." Laic shook his head sadly. "The next thing we knew there was a huge explosion from the arms room. All of the trainees and spectators quickly ran to the scene. We found Ariana buried under a pile of weapons, and Serenu was gone.

"As we tried to pull Ariana out from under the pile, it became clear that in the explosion, a sword had lodged itself in her neck. She had a gaping wound from the nape of her neck to her collarbone. She was bleeding profusely because one of her arteries had been partially severed. She also had numerous other wounds all over her body. She was barely alive. We rushed her to the Leku rooms immediately, using immobilizing spells to keep the sword from moving around as we ran. Lianco was already at the infirmary when I arrived, and he almost fainted at the sight of his dear friend with the sword in her neck and too many other injuries to count.

"Lianco and I did a rapid once-over examination, checking for vital organ damage. Luckily, her major internal systems were intact, but the blood loss was impacting her heart, and the sword had to come out. She had three cracked ribs, two broken neck vertebrae, a broken collarbone, and her left shin was shattered into a dozen pieces. How she survived I really have no idea. The technique we used to fix her was one that had never been used before by any of the Leku present. Up to that point, we had only read about the process, but there was no time to waste.

"The technique required us to stop her heart to halt blood flow, remove the sword, sterilize and heal the neck wound, re-bond her vertebrae, fix her collarbone, and then restart her heart. Her brain could only stay alive for five minutes without oxygenated blood, so we knew we had to move with lightning speed. Between the two of us, we managed to send the right amount of electrical pulses to stall her heart, and our hands flew over her body in a flurry of healing. We had braced her onto a table that flipped up sideways, so that I could work on her back while Lianco attended to her wounded neck and collarbone. It was the most intense process either of us had ever been through, and we managed to get everything done in four minutes. However, we hadn't factored in the level of exhaustion that results from healing that quickly, and we weren't able create enough electrical pulses by the fifth minute to restart her heart. Lianco was angry and anxious, so he wasn't thinking very clearly. His emotions took over, and in a burst of adrenaline, he sent enough electrical pulses into her to kill an elephant. The whole process took almost six minutes, rather than five."

"Is that bad?" Dan asked. Laic looked like he might cry as he continued to tell his account of the story.

"We didn't think so. At first we thought everything was fine. Ariana opened her eyes, recognized us, and spoke a little. We set about fixing the cracked ribs and other minor wounds. After we were finished, we could find no other physical damages, but she did not seem herself.

"Then, after about a week passed, Ariana's eyes began to change color. They faded from their usual electric green to a washed out silvery gray. She freaked out when she saw herself. We assured her that everything would be fine, since we couldn't find evidence that anything else was wrong. We thought it was a symptom of the trauma, and hoped it would undo itself, but the silver eyes stayed. Just when she started getting used to her new eyes, she had another setback. Overnight, her hair turned from its usual raven black to the color of white sand—silvery blonde as you've seen. Her hair still shined like no other, but the Ariana we had known was gone."

"But how?" Dan asked. "How could her eyes and her hair just change like that? I've never heard of anything so strange." Dan had been listening to Laic's story very closely, and I could see that he was moved by the emotional turmoil she had endured.

"You see, we overlooked any damage to her nerves and genetic markers when we investigated the changes. When Lianco administered the large dose of electrical impulses, he did not aim very well, and the electricity affected other areas besides her heart. The pulses traveled through the bloodstream, and collided with her DNA. The electricity was high enough and hot enough that it mutated her chromosomes and damaged her enzymes. In short, we altered her without knowing we were."

"It would be an understatement to say Ariana was upset. For weeks, she couldn't even look at herself in the mirror. Unfortunately, the changes didn't stop there. Her beautiful, milky-white skin faded into a pale, almost translucent version of the original. It was awful to watch, and even harder knowing it was our mistake that caused the change."

"Wow…" was all I could think to say.

"She seems so strong," Dan said sadly.

"She only has Lianco to keep her together now. And you," Laic said.

"Wait, so why was Alita upset?" I asked. Dan rolled his eyes.

"No wonder you've been unsuccessful with guys," my brother chided. "Alita is obviously in love with Lianco. Or at least she's really fond of him." Laic nodded in agreement. I sighed, annoyed at being inexperienced, but it was true that love affairs were not something I'd had much practice with.

A slight movement caught my attention. Alita's hand was slowly curling into a fist though her eyes were still staring straight ahead, unblinking. Laic winked in my direction and motioned for me not to say anything. Then, he continued with his story.

"It is absolutely true that Alita has feelings for Lianco. But I believe those feelings stem from her feelings for his other brother…Serenu."

Alita's eyebrows twitched.

"You see, Alita is a Seiku, a Being with magic. She had access to the Dark Books, and unfortunately, she used that access to help Serenu in his quest to gain dual powers."

Alita's mouth made a small grimace.

"She has always had a thing for the bad boys," Laic smiled.

Alita's other hand twitched.

"Sadly," he continued, "I don't think her infatuation was ever returned. And when Serenu disappeared, Lianco was there. He conveniently filled that emotional void for Alita. He was sympathetic and paid attention to her. And thus, her infatuation for Serenu simply moved from one person to the next."

Laic looked extremely pleased with himself, having so thoroughly answered our questions. I noticed a tiny tear rolling down Alita's cheek as her eyes came back into focus. Laic didn't see her wake up, so he was a little surprised when she stopped any more of his words by putting a firm hand over his mouth.

"I think I can take it from here," she said icily. "But, first, please heal this rut on my face."

Laic's hands moved swiftly and within seconds, the

gash was gone, with barely even a scar to remind us where it had been.

"So I guess you know all about my mortal enemy," Alita said.

"Mortal enemy? Do you mean Ariana? Why do you two have to hate each other?" I said heatedly. Alita raised an eyebrow back at me.

"Weren't you listening to the story?"

Alita

How could I explain this? How could I possibly make them understand? Liz was a natural bookworm, a very smart girl who lived in a world of black and white. No gray areas. No room for exception, just right and wrong. So, how could someone like that understand why I acted the way I did? How what happened, happened? Liz stared expectantly at me, waiting for some kind of answer. Dan looked to the side as if bored, and Laic busied himself with cleaning up the materials he had used for my repair. Frankly, I had no idea why Liz was just staring at me, since I had asked the last question.

"Fine," I said, suddenly angry at the whole situation. I shouldn't have to explain myself to her. She was so new, so naïve, and she didn't know me as well as she thought. "I'm tired of all this drama."

Liz opened her mouth to speak but I was past her and out the door before she could get any words out. No one tried to stop me, and I sent a *thank you* for that via *allreçu* to Laic. I wasn't in love with Lianco. He was a good friend, and someone I greatly respected. But, while everyone thought I was infatuated, the truth was Lianco just reminded me of the person I really loved.

Serenu loved me, too, of that I was sure. He had to. After

all the time we spent together, and all that we had shared, there was no way he couldn't love me. And yet…he had left. He had disappeared to a place I could not follow, no matter how many portals I tried.

It was true that I exposed Serenu to the Dark Books, the black magic that had been sealed away after the Originals discovered the amount of destruction such magic could cause. All the dark magic had been banned from use. Telekinesis, body possession, and the portals themselves were all outlawed because they could be used in ways that hurt the Alliance. The idea that one individual could control the movements and weapons of an entire army using telekinesis put everyone in danger.

I discovered the use of portals on my own after swiping one of the Dark Books. Lianco found out, but he didn't wipe their existence from my memory. Instead, he allowed me to keep the knowledge with the understanding that the portals could become a significant asset if used correctly, and on the right side of a fight.

Historically, evil Beings had been known to use portals for the purposes of chaos and destruction. Their ability to move swiftly and easily from place to place enabled them to take enemies by surprise, which gave them the upper hand in battle. However, Lianco felt I would only use them for the good of the Alliance. I had earned his trust.

*   *   *

181

The Vaults and Archives were often the subject of folklore for young people within the Alliance. A locked door usually meant something valuable was behind it, and the myths and rumors of what might be hidden within ran rampant. Legend had it that the Dark Books lay deep within the Vaults where they were meant to be kept from innocent eyes.

Even I'm not really sure how I got into the Vaults, but once I found myself inside, I scanned the whole place for any treasures worth knowing about, or worth having. I got a hold of one of the smaller, more encyclopedic volumes of the Dark Books before the Neku Keepers of the Vaults discovered I had broken in. The book I managed to escape with didn't have any spells. All it contained was information about the origin and background of Dark magic. I was actually quite proud of my elicit robbery, and presented the book to Serenu in an attempt to show him just how deeply I loved him. Sadly, Serenu was not as pleased with my find as I had hoped. He wanted a book of spells, a 'how-to' of forbidden magic to use to his own advantage. However, he took the knowledge the book offered and set to work trying to create his own spells.

Several times, his spells actually worked. He succeeded in causing a body to be possessed, and taught a set of bones how to wield a sword, but the spells were usually short-lived. He could not hold the magic for long periods of time; eventually, the spells dissipated and he would have to start from scratch. He practiced whenever he could, usually after training sessions and late at night. But, he was not a Seiku like his father. He had no natural magical abilities, and working with as volatile a subject as magic ruined him.

Once Serenu failed his Roku qualifying test, his emotions spun into complete turmoil. He had failed the test that would have granted him membership into the Alliance and finally cemented his place in the Realm. He had lost everything he had worked for in a matter of hours, and he was as upset as I had ever seen him. He was in no condition to perform any spell, much less one of Dark magic.

Ariana chased after him, to console him I suppose. Serenu believed he was worthy of Alliance membership, and went overboard trying to demonstrate his abilities to Ariana. Demonstrating his newfound 'power' to her in his agitated state made his experimental magic backfire, and he gravely injured one of his best friends. Lianco believed Serenu disappeared immediately after the incident, but in reality, he came to me first. I was the last person he talked to before he disappeared completely. I never saw him after that, even when he was captured and thrown into the Abyss.

*   *   *

I realized I had made my way to my apartment from the Leku sector while I was lost myself in memories. The small metal door flung open at my command and I threw myself onto my bed. I looked around at my richly decorated room. I had used the portals to my personal advantage to bring back exotic relics and treasures from all over the world. But hey, what Lianco didn't know wouldn't hurt him. My apartment was decorated with all the beautiful things I loved—gemstones from the diamond mines of South Africa, plants from the Amazon, ancient works of literature from England, and the best furniture from New York. However, none of my treasures could console me. Not one of them masked the loss I felt deep down in my heart. I had only one true love, and always would, no matter how far away he was.

Dan

Liz was really angry after the episode with Alita, so I gave her time to calm down. Once Laic was sure Liz was over it, he agreed to start working with us in the morning on our Leku skills.

We already knew a fair amount about Leku history from him and Lianco, so he kept that part to a quick overview and then began to teach us how to heal. Laic was a good instructor—calm and matter of fact. He taught us how to clean wounds, heal scrapes, disperse bruises, and even reattach limbs. Some of it was pretty gross, but most of the techniques were fascinating. Both of us were immensely intrigued by what were learning.

Liz learned quickly; she picked up the rhythms and movements of the circulatory system much faster than I did, but that was her nature. She was smarter than me. It took me awhile just to learn the patterns and pathways of how blood moves through the body.

The entire Leku training took roughly eight hours. The only thing we didn't learn was the technique that had been used to heal Ariana. Laic touched on parts of it, such as how to restart the heart, but when we asked if we could practice the procedure, Laic refused to let us try. He didn't want to risk another situation like Ariana's.

As training came to a close, Laic pulled out
a small, marble box and gave us our Leku
marking, signifying the completion of our
Leku training. The minute it was over, we
crashed. Liz and I barely made it back to our
apartment, and basically stumbled into our respective
beds fully clothed. (At least I did. Knowing Liz, she probably
went through her normal bedtime routine before crawling
under the covers.)

Leku

We knew all too well that we needed our sleep because
the our toughest training, magic, was coming up next. The
teacher was the one person in the Alliance who still hated
Rokenan with a passion: the Seiku Master.

*　　*　　*

I took a deep breath and stole a quick glance at Liz. Her
face was pale and she had that worry line on her forehead
between her eyebrows. I also noticed her hands were shaking
slightly, the same as mine. *Good*, I thought. *At least I'm not
the only one who's nervous.* The big doors to the Seiku sector
loomed in front of us.

"These people definitely have a thing for big doors," I
joked weakly. Liz responded with a half-hearted chuckle and
together we pushed the bronze monsters open.

As we walked in, I expected to be greeted by the crusty,
wrinkled Master, but instead I saw Alita's smiling face waiting
for us. I could feel Liz stiffen the slightest bit beside me, but
Alita seemed like her old self; the argument appeared to have

been forgotten. That, or she was much better at hiding her feelings than my sister.

"Orion bailed, which isn't surprising, so I will be your only assistant during this training," she said and smiled. "Master Kailen isn't likely to wait long," her smile turned somewhat apologetic, "so look around quickly." I had anticipated a dusty, dark room with fiery cauldrons and old books, but the Seiku sector's training facility was quite modern. The walls were pale, bathed in an undistinguishable color somewhere between white, taupe, and beige. Black stone pillars dotted the room, each engraved with ancient gold carvings. In the background, there was a distinct whirring sound that I couldn't place. Through an archway across the training room, I could see another area filled with very old books, so old that the barely perceptible smoke hanging in the doorway was probably the dust from their pages.

Though quite small on the surface compared to the giant Roku training room, the Seiku lair was bigger than the eye could see. While the Roku sector was completely open to the front, with four tiers coming off a large main room, the Seiku's training facility was comprised of a series of interlocking rooms, connected by a matrix of winding corridors. *Big doors, twists and turns,* I thought to myself. *These people really enjoy the ancient theme.*

Alita stood carefully on top of a huge stone circle in the middle of the room, and we watched as she stepped lightly around the edges in a pattern that I could not follow. With the last step, the circle slid open to reveal a downward spiraling stone staircase.

"Normally we use the chutes, but this is a special case," she said with a shrug. I looked around for what she was talking about and discovered the source, or sources, of the whirring noises I'd been hearing. All around the room, Seikus young and old popped up or disappeared into square holes about three feet by three feet. The holes looked like they were made of stone. I watched a young Seiku girl pop up from a nearby chute, step lightly onto the ground and walk out the main doors.

"I guess they're like elevators," Liz whispered to me.

"Exactly," Alita smiled. "They are a Seiku invention. There's an up and a down chute right next to each other, with a total of eight sets of chutes."

"So, the whirring noise is…the chutes?" I asked.

"Well, actually what you hear is the wind in the chutes. Seikus use a spell to force enough air under their feet to propel them upward, or to slowly lower them. Now, come on, we'd better hurry. We have a lot to do."

Alita led us down the spiral staircase, which progressively lit up as we descended. The stairs wound down past level after level of open rooms and training areas. We must have passed ten floors before the stairs finally flattened out at the very bottom. I leaned over to Liz and softly said, "No wonder they use the chutes. That was a long way down."

"Wait here," Alita whispered. She stepped through the open doorway across from us. I used the opportunity to look around the room, which looked more like a basement storage area than anything else. Compared to the intricate designs and layout on the top floor, the bottom was very plain. The walls and floor were all dirt, and the room itself wasn't much bigger than my dorm room at UT.

Alita reappeared with a very old man on her arm. He looked even older than Guana, which I didn't think was possible. But I felt there was more to him than what I saw. Beneath his pocked and wrinkled skin, an electricity pulsed. Something about him felt alive, unfinished. His face was drawn into a look of disdain, and I remembered the warnings about his utter hatred for Rokenan.

The Master struggled with Alita's arm until she let go, and he walked unsteadily toward us. Up close, I noticed the old man's eyes were milky and glazed over. It was obvious that he was blind.

"So," the Master said with a crackling voice, as though his words were laced with fire. "You are Zoran and Zaria."

I looked over at Liz and nodded. I quickly realized my mistake as I felt a stinging blow to the side of my head. I jerked around at the unexpected strike.

"Look at me when I talk to you, *boy*," Master Kailen said angrily.

"How did you know I wasn't looking at you? You're—"

"Blind? Being without sight is not a disability. After so many years, I do not have to see to know; nature has a way of compensating for that loss. My other senses have taken over in place of my sight. Every movement of your body disrupts the air, and I can hear it. Every breath taken, every hand gesture given, even a slight turn of the head are all as plain to me as if I had seen them with someone else's eyes. And you, clumsy boy, make a *lot* of noise just standing there." My jaw went slack at his abruptness. "Do we understand each other?"

"Y-Yes," I stammered. "I mean, yes sir."

"Good. Now, as you've probably been told, I don't like you two."

"Master!" Alita interrupted. "Now is not the time to—"

"Silence! My grandfather was the leader of the Revolution, and his hatred for Rokenan was as much an inheritance to me as his genes. I am the sole remaining Seiku who remembers and who bears a complete loathing of your sector. I will take no mercy on you just because Lianco says I should. If you are true Rokenan, you should have no problem absorbing the material. But it will not be given easily." He smirked at his own twisted joke.

Before we could grasp his meaning, his hands blurred around his body. Water droplets formed next to his palms, then turned to icy shards which shot toward the ground. At the same time, balls of fire emerged from his hands, ricocheted off the walls and disappeared into his palms. A strong wind blew through the room, sending Liz's hair into a curly cloud around her face. The ground shook roughly, and small square pieces of dirt from the earthy floor rose into orbit, encircling the Master's head.

"Water, fire, air, earth," he said through the commotion. "Each of these elements have hundreds of spells connected to them. But to use the spells to your advantage, you must first understand each of the elements you are dealing with." All at once, the conjured elements dissipated into thin air. "This is your first lesson. Master the elements, if you can. Then we will proceed from there."

Without another word he disappeared through the open doorway. Liz stared at me dumbly, as if I was supposed to know what to do next. I shrugged my shoulders and we both looked at Alita for help.

"'Master them? How do we even conjure the elements?" Liz asked.

"You pull them from your surroundings," Alita said simply. When she could see that neither of us had any idea what she was talking about, Alita explained herself. "Focus your mind, just like you learned to do in your Roku training," she said. "Picture what you want to happen and then say the word. It's that easy. Here, sit down."

The three of us sat in a circle on the earthen floor. "Picture a perfect square of dirt being cut from the ground in front of you. Then, picture it floating up in front of your face. Form the image in your mind and then say the word, *terra*."

"What's that?" Liz asked.

"It's the word for earth in the ancient language. It's also the command that makes it happen," she said.

"Oh, right."

I tried to picture a block of dirt rising from the ground. Then, softly, I gave the command. "*Terra.*" The only thing I conjured was a tiny clump of dirt that fell right into my lap. Great. I heard the word "*terra*" from beside me and looked over at Liz. Floating in the air in front of her was a perfect square of earth, not a foot from her nose.

"Typical," I muttered. She smirked at me and Alita chuckled.

"Try again, Dan, but this time concentrate all of your energies. You can't let your mind wander. You have to really mean it when you command something like the earth to move," Alita said supportively.

I took a deep breath and closed my eyes to try again. I cleared my mind and thought about absolutely nothing. Then, I pictured a square piece of earth like Liz's, and repeated the conjuring word. When I opened my eyes, a perfect cube of earth floated in front of my face.

"See? Just like that." Alita grinned.

Liz

I laughed out loud as balls of fire and water circled my hands in a dizzying display. Alita had shown us how to draw on the moisture in the air for *aqua*, use the earth's heat for *ignis*, and propel the wind using *aere*. We had successfully mastered the art of conjuring all four elements. Once we understood the basic processes, Alita introduced us to the more complex spells—the fun stuff.

We learned how to shoot streams of fire, suspend huge amounts of water, create clay figures, and whip up surprise wind attacks. The solid, dirt room acted as a fantastic barrier, or cage, for our practice since nothing could catch on fire or be totally drenched. As we honed our skills, Dan created water men and I created fire men, and then we watched as they dissolved each other in mock battles.

Distracted by our own amusement, we didn't notice Master Kailen appear in the doorway, scowling. It wasn't until Alita cleared her throat to alert us that we noticed his presence.

"Well," he crackled, "that was fast. Too fast, I think."

He glared at us with blank eyes, a gaze that was probably supposed to intimidate us, but his disdain only amused us at this point. Our new-found knowledge had made us significantly braver. In a huff, Kailen disappeared again, this time drawing on the earthen floor to fill the doorway behind him, until it was completely solid. We did not see the old man again after that. Alita, Seiku prodigy that she was, taught us everything else there was to know.

We learned countless spells, like how to manipulate metal, electricity, light, and weather. The coolest thing we learned was how to bend the light waves around us to make ourselves invisible. Not only would that come in handy during a battle, but it would be awesome to use at college.

Creating storms and tornadoes fell under weather training. In the realm of electricity, we learned how to create an electric shock so big that it could blackout half the continental United States (though we didn't test it). We also discovered how to create a movable, malleable, fairly comfortable metal suit of armor when nanocloth was unavailable. When we had learned all we needed, Alita smiled.

"You are true Rokenan. No ordinary Seiku could have absorbed that much in one day." Alita produced a small, glass box from behind her, and administered our Seiku marks, completing the set of four on our wrists. "You now hold the knowledge of almost every spell ever created. There is one more I can teach you, if you want to learn it."

SEIKU

She held her left palm out, facing up to the ceiling and parallel to the floor. We stared as tiny bits of blue light gathered in it. The blue specks kept coming, pulled from the room around us and possibly from further away, until they formed a small ball of light. The ball hovered above her palm. As it rotated, we could see the various shades of blue within the ball. The aura was mesmerizing. We were even more surprised when the sphere began growing until it was the size of a tennis ball, floating just above Alita's palm.

"With this," Alita said, "I can step through a wall into anyplace in the world."

"That's how she got me," Dan announced. "Some door thing appears from that," he pointed at the ball of light, "and you step through it to a whole new place." Dan waved his arms around for emphasis. To show us how it worked, Alita reached her hand out and put it against the dirt wall.

Suddenly, purple sparks filled the room. Alita cried out in pain, but I was blinded by the bright light. Dan grabbed my arm and pulled me to him, protecting me with his size. When the light finally dimmed, the scene that lay before us was devastating.

Alita was motionless on the floor with bright red blood seeping out from under her hair. Screaming and shaken, I stared at the place where my friend lay, mortally wounded. Then, I noticed someone else in the room—another me. My body, my hair, my face—another me stood across the room, laughing. Just like in my dream. I tried to speak but fear kept any words from coming out.

"Who the hell are you?" Dan growled at the fake me.

"Wouldn't you like to know?" The thing spoke with my voice and the face gave a familiar smirk, but I could sense something was off. Then my duplicate threw back its head and let go a high, giggling laugh that was nothing like my own.

"Oops," it said, still in my voice, "still working out the kinks."

As we watched, the imposter began to vibrate and shimmer. The face and body started to change. The brown curls turned jet-black and straightened out. The arms got more muscular, the chest bigger, and the waist curvier.

"Oh my god," I breathed as the face finally changed. "Brooke?"

"Actually, sweetie," my roommate's high, cheerleader voice chimed, "it's *Violet*."

"Brooke?" Dan echoed. "Head cheerleader Brooke from Northbrook High? Brooke, the Hottie with a Body, Brooke?" Dan was at a loss for intelligence, thanks to his unresolved infatuation with the Brooke he remembered.

"Yes, Dan, that Brooke. I was her. And I see you're still as dumb as you've always been."

"What happened to your hair?" I wondered aloud.

"I dyed it," she retorted. "Blonde was too, well, too blonde. Plus, this color brings out my eyes, don't you think?."

"It looks just like Al—"

"Don't even go there," she warned. "Someone said I would look better with dark hair, and I agreed, so I changed it."

"Speaking of which, where have you been anyway? And what the hell did you do to Al—"

"*Don't* say her name," she snapped. "I just came to collect a little something and then I will be on my way." Violet held up a glowing blue sphere, which was beginning to change color, to purple.

"That's Alita's—"

"What did I tell you about saying that name?" Violet shouted. "God...*sweetie*, for someone so smart, you can act so dumb." She laughed at her own joke. "That little tart over there won't be needing this and I know someone who does."

"What did you do to her, you bitch?" I said through my teeth.

"Oh, a little of this, a little of that. I didn't want to kill her, just knock her out for a while. I mean, seriously, what chance does a mere Seiku have against someone like me?" Violet smirked.

"Take Alita to Laic," I whispered to Dan urgently.

"But I can't just leave you with her."

"Go. I'll be fine. This is my fight."

"Actually, I'm not planning to fight you," came a knife-like response from across the room. Violet held up one, perfectly manicured hand. "Just did my nails and I don't want to break one. I got what I came for so now I'm going. Okay? Bye-bye."

"You take one step and I'll tear you to shreds," I snapped. Dan was out the door with Alita in his arms before I had ended my sentence. Violet focused her stony, purple eyes on me.

"Would you look at that?" she taunted. "Little miss Liz has a backbone after all. You think you can take me down, sweetie? I doubt it; in fact, I dare you to try." Purple sparks gathered around her other hand as she prepared for a fight.

"Why are you here?" I asked icily, stalling as I focused my

energies. I had never fought an actual person. All our training had been simulated, so true combat was sure to be more challenging.

"It's like I said. I'm running an errand, and I've completed my job. I don't have the time to play games with a newbie." Turning, Violet shoved her hand against the wall behind her and stepped back as a purple, shimmering door grew from the spot. "Catch you later!" she laughed as one foot stepped into the glow.

Before I knew what I was doing, a bolt of lightning shot out of my hand and hit her directly between the shoulder blades. I could see a tremor reverberate through her body as the back of the black shirt she wore was singed to nothing. She stopped in her tracks, and it seemed as though time froze for a few seconds. When she wheeled around, her eyes were on fire and purple radiated from both her hands. I thought about running, but my legs were as heavy as lead and my feet seemed rooted to the ground with fear.

"You must think you're so clever," she mocked in a terrifying voice. "I bet you've never fought anyone in your life. Well get ready, sweetie, because this will be like nothing you've ever experienced."

She raised her hands to strike, then suddenly stopped. She closed her eyes, and was suddenly silent. She turned her head left and right, eyes still closed, as if she was hearing something I couldn't. Slowly the two purple glows disappeared. The episode lasted the better part of a minute before her eyes flipped open again.

"This isn't over," she warned before turning on her heel

and leaping through the door behind her. Once she had gone, the door shimmered and disappeared.

Partly relieved and partly more furious with her than ever, I sank heavily to the ground. A million questions ran through my head. Where had she been? Where was she now? Why did she want what the blue sphere Alita had? Most importantly, whose errand was she running?

*   *   *

I flew down the long corridor, running faster than I had ever run before, thanks to the wind I created at my back and under my feet. I knew Dan could handle getting Alita to the healing rooms, so I ran toward the one person who should know what had happened, if he didn't already. Lianco looked up from his desk with a start when I ran into his office unannounced. Ariana, who was sitting on the couch reading, also turned with a surprised look on her face.

"Alita…Violet…blood…sphere…door…gone!" I said frantically, my hands flailing around in an effort to describe what my words left out. Adrenaline coursed through me and my brain couldn't compose complete sentences. Lianco didn't say a word. He just stood up behind his desk, watching me, waiting for another outburst.

"Liz?" Ariana approached me cautiously, one hand outstretched as if she thought I might be dangerous. "Liz, slow down. Tell us what happened."

"Violet's back and she hurt Alita while we were finishing our Seiku training. She took the little glowing sphere and she had dyed her hair and she changed into me and then disappeared!" I tried to slow down, but the words came out of my mouth so quickly that they didn't make sense, so I was glad when Lianco jumped in to figure it out.

"Violet is back?" I nodded. "And, Alita is hurt?" I nodded again. "Where is she now? Is she safe?" I answered his question with a nod. "Speak, Liz. Tell me about Alita."

"Alita's hurt, something happened to her head. Dan's taken her to the healing rooms, to Laic."

"And Violet took the glowing sphere?"

"Yes."

"She got a hold of the portal sphere…" he mused.

"Portal sphere?" Ariana asked, confused. "I'm not Seiku, but even I've never heard of such a thing."

"I will tell you about it later," Lianco said hurriedly. "What did you mean about Violet changing into you? And, something about her hair?"

"Violet looks exactly like Alita now! Her long blonde hair is dyed black and cut so it brushes her shoulders. Before that, she transformed herself to look just like me. When we first saw her, when she first appeared, she looked like me. Even her voice was the same as mine. It was like looking in the mirror. Then, my body just dissolved away and hers took its place."

"Mirroring," Lianco said decisively.

"Portals? Mirroring? Where is all of this coming from?" Ariana cried in frustration.

"It is Dark magic, Ariana. It was hidden away in the Vaults, where no one should have gotten to it. Only one person ever has."

"You mean Serenu?" Ariana whispered.

Lianco shook his head. "No, I mean Alita."

"What?" Ariana and I both said in shock.

"Alita was helping Master Kailen with Seiku documents in the Neku Archives when she found an alternate entrance to the Vaults. She did not even know what they were at the time, but her curiosity made her enter," Lianco explained.

"But everyone knows the Vaults!" Ariana said, exasperated. "Many people have access to them. It would be too easy for Dark magic to fall into the wrong hands if it was stored in the Vaults."

"Trust me," Lianco said, "the Neku library has areas most people have never seen. The Dark magic has its own, entirely separate wing, far from the public Vaults. The area is quite secure. How Alita got in without detection is a mystery, but once she was inside, she figured out the importance of the books there. Out of curiosity, she opened a book and saw that it contained information about Dark magic. Paging through it, she discovered the portal spell. The portal sphere can conjure a door which will take her anywhere in the world. She is the only one who can do it in all of the Alliance."

I cleared my throat. "Actually, she's not."

I closed my eyes, concentrating on pulling the pieces of the universe together for my door. When I opened them again, a ball of yellow light the size of a ping-pong ball floated in my hand. I stole a glance at Lianco and the shocked expression on his face was priceless. I walked to the nearest wall, the ball of light growing bigger with every step. I had to prove to the two of them what I could do. It was all riding on this, whether or not the magic was good, whether or not it ended with the same result as Alita's. I thrust my hand against the wall and felt the jolt in my hand as my magic connected with the solid surface. The yellow light washed over the stones and formed a shining rectangle more beautiful than any fireworks I had ever seen. The energy that had come out of my hand, created by me, bent space and time so that I had the ability to transport anywhere.

I turned around with a look of pure joy. Ariana's mouth was hanging wide open, and Lianco looked like he might throw up.

"She...taught you...that?" he managed to say.

"Well, yes," I replied. "But she got hurt showing us how it works."

"When I get my hands on her, I swear—"

"Lianco, don't be angry at her. She said it would come in handy sometime," I explained, holding him back as he tried to make a beeline for the door. "She wouldn't tell us what we'd need it for, just that it would come in handy."

Lianco fumed for a moment. "We are going to the Leku. Now."

Lianco

Ariana had her hand firmly on my arm as we walked to the Leku sector. Her intention was to calm me, but it was a futile attempt. I was so angry my whole body was shaking, and I had no outlet for the anger because Alita was hurt, maybe even unconscious. But damn it, Alita had been warned. She had strict instructions from me not to share her knowledge of Dark magic. She knew what was at stake, and yet she had demonstrated some of the forbidden skills to the last two people who would (or should) ever need them.

What was she thinking? To muster some amount of self-control, I paced down the hallway in slow, measured strides, half dragging poor Ariana.

You are in so much trouble, I sent out to Alita as we neared my sector. I knew I would not get a response, but once I saw her, I was sure she heard me.

Laic and Dan stood over her, holding her down on the table. She was struggling to get up, thrashing left and right, trying to escape their strong hands. All of her efforts against them stopped the moment she saw me in the doorway.

"You," I said menacingly, advancing on the three of them, but focusing my gaze directly on Alita. "You are in so—"

"Lianco please. She has a head injury," Laic warned as he stepped between us. "Do not interfere with my work. You should not push her. You know what effects stress can have in such a case."

"I can explain, Lianco!" Alita protested.

"Save it!" I ordered. My attempts at restraint dissipated as my temper took over. "I was *very* clear with you on the use of Dark magic. I gave you one instruction after I found out about your adventures in the Vaults, only one! And you disobeyed me! You broke your promise…and in doing so, you shared that knowledge with the two most important and most vulnerable people in this whole situation!"

"But I—"

"I don't want to hear it! You broke your word and that comes with a price. You must be punished."

"Lianco, please let me—"

"I have not decided exactly what the appropriate punishment will be, but when I do—"

"LET ME SPEAK!" Alita screamed, stunning me into silence. "I realized I was taking a chance when I showed them. But I had a hunch their unique senses and skills could help us find Serenu if they could use the portals," Alita explained. "They're Rokenan, right? So they have more power than any one of us. That means they might be the only ones who can figure out some way to open a portal to the Unknown. I have never been able to, and believe me, I've tried. Perhaps they can go in and come back in one piece." Alita let her words settle into the silence.

"But Serenu came back," Dan said slowly. "And now he's got the Book, so we won't be the only ones who have figured it out."

"That might be where Violet went, too," Liz added.

"True. But neither of them would be expecting you two to show up there," Alita said with a small smile. "They have no idea of the strength of your powers."

"Do you realize the risk you are suggesting?" I asked. "The Legends are our only hope should things go badly. Anyway, exactly how are they supposed to go about getting to the Unknown? Serenu knows how because *you* gave him the basic information and he worked the rest out himself over time. But, I am not positive he is using a portal."

"I'm not sure either. I'm not even certain they can create a portal to the Unknown, but I have an idea about how to try," she replied. "Remember, Lianco, we are in a desperate situation, and I realize that you're still the boss. What I am suggesting is only based on intuition, but I think it's worth attempting."

"Why don't we try it?" Liz suggested confidently. She was obviously ready to take on a more significant role.

"Only with Lianco's blessing." Alita stood up and turned to me for approval. Ariana nodded as if to add her endorsement. I was outnumbered and out of other options.

"I cannot say I am happy about it…but it does seem logical to try. We are in a desperate situation. I realize extreme measures may be our only hope." I turned to Liz and Dan and said, "You must understand the tremendous risk you are taking. Traveling to the Unknown is very dangerous. The place itself is disturbing. Most who travel there never return, so you need to be on alert at all times. You must watch out for each other."

Alita gestured for the two of them to stand next to her. "I think the only way to accomplish this is for each of you to conjure your own portal while picturing the Unknown, and then combine the portals," she said softly.

"I understand the portal thing, but how are we supposed to picture the Unknown?" Liz asked. "We've never been there, nor have we seen anything that describes it."

"Just think about it as layers and layers of clouds. A dense, gray fog that is difficult to see through. Picture yourself in a fog that would leave anyone aimlessly lost."

The amount of concentration Liz and Dan were putting in was visible on their faces. The rest of us stood as still as possible, almost praying for results. Pretty soon, a small yellow ball of light began to form in Liz's hand and a blue one appeared in Dan's. They looked up at Alita, and moving very slowly, they put their hands closer together.

"Wait!" Alita cried. "Don't join them there. Transfer them to the wall at the same moment."

In unison they turned toward the wall and did exactly as Alita instructed. The result was impressive. Yellow and blue light spread across the surface in various patterns, much like Liz's single portal had done before. However, this new door was massive. The combined lights continued to spread until almost the entire wall was a shimmering blur of pale green light. Laic, Alita, Ariana, and I were squinting into the light to see if the other side was what we hoped (and feared) it would be. Dan and Liz were caught up in the light, almost glowing from it. Tilting my head back and forth, I could see vague images behind the shimmering brightness. There was something there, something gray moving back and forth behind the green.

"That is the Unknown." I whispered aloud, amazed that these two young people had managed to conjure an opening to such an unreachable place.

I was unable to finish my thought because the green light began to move faster. It transformed into a whirling vortex that seemed to be sucking in the light and bending the wall inward. As we all stood there dumbfounded, the green light began to disappear into the gray, taking Liz and Dan in with it. They must have felt the pull because both of them turned and reached out for us with panicked expressions.

"Grab them!" I shouted, lunging forward to clutch their outstretched arms.

Laic and Ariana lunged as well, but none of us could get to them in time. In a matter of seconds, the portal had changed forms and taken them in. They had disappeared into the depths of the Unknown…possibly forever.

Forty-Four

Dan

When I opened my eyes, I couldn't see anything. Not that I was blind; no, the place we were in was one big gray nothing as far as the eye could see. At first I thought we had landed in a foggy, volcanic crater. Lying there, I could feel the ground below me was hard, but crumbly to the touch, and the air was cold with no breeze. I sat up slowly, trying to take in my surroundings. What did I find? More nothing. Liz groaned and sat up beside me, rubbing the back of her head. She, too, was looking around and though I couldn't see her clearly just two feet away, I could tell by her face that the stark surroundings were causing her a similar confusion.

"What the heck was *that?*" she asked.

"That was a portal ass-kicking," I muttered. "Any clue where we are?"

"Brrr. Well, it's cold, and it's foggy, it's gray, and it's deserted…"

"Thank you, Captain Obvious."

"What are you, a fourth grader?" Liz asked.

"I know you are, but what am I?" I couldn't stop myself from blurting out a childish come back. Maybe I had hit my head harder than I first thought.

"Shut up, Dan," she said as she rolled her eyes. "Whatever we did with the portals must have warped your brain. All kidding aside, do you really not know where we are?"

Suddenly, it hit me. "You think we made it to the Unknown?"

"Unfortunately, yes," she sighed, "I think we're here."

"Wow. Ok, so, what happens now?" I asked.

"For once, I have no idea. I guess our fearless leader didn't cover that before we conjured the portals."

We sat there on the cold, hard ground for what seemed like hours, waiting for inspiration as to what our plan should be. Occasionally, a dim light would barely illuminate the gray fog around us, only to disappear once more. Nothing was everywhere, and everywhere was nothing.

I leaned back with my fingers interlaced behind my head, figuring I might as well take a nap. It had been a long week and I was mentally and physically worn out. Suddenly, a voice sounded in my head.

How does it feel to be lost?

Startled, I sat up quickly, and looked all around for the source of the voice. It couldn't have been Liz, as it was clearly a man's voice. I turned to ask her anyway, and as I did, the voice spoke again.

A little nervous? Maybe even afraid?

"Who are you?" I said into the gray fog. "Where are you?" Liz looked at me like I had lost my mind, but my eyes continued to scan the periphery. I could feel the intensity of her stare, so I turned and said, "What? You don't hear anything?"

"Hear anything?" she said. "There's nothing to hear! This place is beyond empty."

Oh, how sad. Your beloved sister doesn't believe you. But then, she's always thought of you as the lesser twin, right?

"Shut up!" I said.

"I didn't say anything!" Liz declared angrily.

"Not you!!" I cried. I waited for the voice again but it didn't come. Instead, Liz began to look around frantically. She pointed at her ear and mouthed '*I hear it now.*'

"Wait a minute," she said after a little while. "I know that voice. I've heard it somewhere before." Liz closed her eyes and tapped her temple, searching for the answer as I had seen her do so many times before. When Liz was stumped, she sifted through thoughts and memories in her head that were apparently filed as well as any computer's records. After a minute or two, she looked up with an unreadable expression on her face.

"Of course. Serenu," she whispered.

A sinister laugh sounded through the gloom, and we watched in fear and fascination as a shadowy figure appeared. He walked toward us with purposeful, confident strides. His dark hair fell over his eyes, swaying slightly with his movements. He was dressed simply, mostly in black, looking every bit the bad guy he was purported to be. To put it plainly, his sudden appearance in this desolate place was terrifying to say the least. This was like our worst nightmare come true. Liz's mouth opened and closed several times, but she was so frightened she was unable to make any words. I reached over to take her hand, determined to be the strong one, just as I had resolved a few days before.

"Dan and Liz, I presume?" he said. Neither of us moved.

Neither of us said a word. I'm not sure we even blinked. I realized we probably should have stood up as he approached, because standing over us put him in a position of power, but I don't think either of us could have stood at that moment. How such a relatively gentle voice came out of such a sinister person was beyond me.

Seconds passed and no one spoke. A tiny smile played about his lips. "Or perhaps you would prefer I called you Zoran and Zaria?"

My back straightened as my instincts kicked in. The gentle voice became loaded with sarcasm, and I had had enough.

"What do you want?" I replied sharply. My fourth grade mannerisms were bubbling up again, and the words came out before I could stop them. My childish retort was not lost on him either.

"Don't be afraid, little Dan," he said with a smirk. "I simply want to know how the two of you managed to get here."

"Shouldn't you already know?" Liz asked, finally finding her voice. "This seems to be your domain."

"*Should* I? Yes, I should know. Do I? Unfortunately, I do not." His once calm voice took on a strained tone.

"Why? Don't you keep watch over the perimeters of this realm?" I asked with a twinge of my own sarcasm. "I mean, Lianco—"

"I am quite aware that my brother can monitor the boundaries of the Unknown!" Serenu practically shouted as he cut me off. "I'm sorry to say it doesn't work both ways. Apparently, I am not as gifted as he. At least in that skill."

Silence fell over the three of us. I kicked myself inside for not being able to think of a snappier retort. Should we rush him and try to take him down? Would any of the skills we had learned from the Masters be enough against him? As I sat there racking my brain for a plan, Liz abruptly stood up with fire in her eyes.

"Where's Brooke?" she demanded angrily.

"Brooke?" Serenu echoed. "Who's Brooke?"

"Okay, Violet! Whatever! Where is she? I have some unfinished business with her."

Serenu chuckled. "I haven't seen Violet for days...not that it's any of your business."

"So, she's not in the Unknown," Liz mumbled to herself.

"What business do you have with Violet?" Serenu asked.

"She hurt Alita," Liz replied. Incredibly, Liz's comment made Serenu freeze. His face changed and I thought he looked, well, pained. He backed up several paces until he was barely visible through the fog around us. I couldn't tell if Liz noticed, but she continued. "Violet hurt Alita and we still don't know if she's okay. I want to make sure she doesn't hurt anyone else." Liz's fingers clenched into fists, her fingernails digging into her palms. "Besides, it's all your fault Alita got hurt. You're the one who sent Violet to do that."

"To do what?"

"To steal the stupid portal!"

"What portal?"

"Aghh!" Liz yelled in frustration. "For someone who acts so tough, you sure are an idiot. Don't you understand? It's your fault! You sent Violet to get the portal, and in the process she nearly killed Alita!"

Serenu was calm and mocking before, but he suddenly became the fourth grader. "I didn't send anyone to do anything, and if Alita is hurt, it's no one's fault but your own," he countered.

"What? How can you say that? Alita is our friend." Angry tears streamed down Liz's face, for her friend, for the situation, for the helplessness she obviously felt in the moment.

"What I mean is, if neither of you had been born, none of this would have happened."

That was the last straw for me. My sister was having a screaming match with the very person who had gotten us in this whole weird situation, and now he was blaming her. I was suddenly shaking with anger at this Serenu person for a lot of reasons: for forcing us into this strange predicament, for his sarcastic comments, and for making my sister cry...

"Look!" I said, standing up and breaking into stride, headed straight for him. "I don't know what your game is, but Violet clearly implied that you were the one who sent her. You told her to dye her hair, and you sent her to get the portal, you son of a bitch! So don't throw this back on us. It's time you faced up to your own demons." I reached my hand out to grab his neck, but before my outstretched hand could reach him, his dark form dissipated into the smoky mist.

My fingers closed around nothing, as if he had never been there. "What the hell?" I said, as the fog settled back into place.

"He's gone," Liz breathed.

"Not gone. Moved," came the mocking voice from our right.

I was infuriated by how amused he seemed about the whole situation. I was ready for a fight, and he was using magic to keep me away from him. I was tensing up to launch another tackling blow, when a low rumble sounded out through the emptiness.

"Oh, my," Serenu's voice said through the fog. "You seem to have woken dear old dad."

"*Dad?* It can't be," Liz breathed. "That means Loki's alive?"

"Of course he's alive. Why wouldn't he be? You can survive much longer here in the Unknown than you can in the Realm. But then, you kids wouldn't know anything about that. Now, if you'll excuse me, I have to be on my way. But, if you'd be so kind…"

Our bodies began moving on their own. Our hands rose in front of us and balls of light suddenly appeared in both our palms. Somehow he was controlling us, controlling our powers. *Body possession*, I thought. *Well, it's better than killing us.*

*For now. But how will we return to the others? He's using our portals…*Liz's voice sounded in my head. I turned and stared at her, unable to process what had just happened.

"You are of much more use to me alive than dead, children," Serenu snorted in response to our shocked expressions.

I was trying to locate the source of his voice so I could go after him, but before I could get a fix on it, the combined portal had been formed and we were catapulted through it.

*   *   *

I sat up, rubbing my head where I had hit it on something hard. I found myself staring at the white topped counters of the Leku sector, before realizing that was where we must have 'landed.' Traveling through space like that was confusing, so I took a minute to shake it off when I saw Laic, Lianco, Alita, and Ariana walking toward me.

"That was fast," Laic said.

"Fast?" Liz sat up beside me, rubbing her nose. "We were gone for forever."

"You just went through the portal about a second and a half ago," Lianco countered with a frown. "You went in through that wall." He pointed across the room. Liz and I stared at each other.

"We went in over there and came out over here? And you're saying it's just been a second or two?" I asked, perplexed.

"Yes," Ariana replied. "Hardly long enough for us to spin around."

"That could explain what he said about people living longer there..." Liz mused.

"He said? 'He' who?" Lianco asked nervously.

"Serenu," I grimaced. "He was there. We saw him." Ariana put a delicate hand to her mouth. "And I would say the Alliance needs to be prepared for anything."

"Anything?" Lianco whispered. "Why do you say that?"

Liz looked seriously at the group. "Because Loki is alive."

Forty-Five

Liz

I was already tired from all the training we'd been through recently and the weird and wild trip to the Unknown, yet we were once again on one of our fast-paced sprints to Lianco's office. *Seems like with all their powers, these Beings would find a way to travel that didn't require quite so much running,* I thought to myself. I noticed that we lined up in the same way we always did, almost the exact same order, like a military regiment. Somewhere along the way, Orion and Darien joined up with us, taking their usual positions at the back.

"Wait here," Lianco called over his shoulder as we neared his office door. "I have to run in for something quickly." The rest of us stood around as he darted in, grabbed something gold and shiny off of his desk, and darted back out. He set a quick pace as we took off.

"Where are we going?" I whispered breathily to Ariana as she ran beside me.

"Roku," she answered. "Hopefully all of us can fit in there."

She was quiet the rest of the way to Roku (my favorite of the four sectors). Not a single sound came from within the great doors, so I was shocked when they opened to reveal a huge crowd gathered inside. The entire Alliance, or what I could only assume to be the entire Alliance, was seated throughout the expanse of the Roku sector. The lower level and all four tiers were covered with people and creatures of all shapes and sizes, with a space cleared in the middle of the ground floor that was obviously meant for the arriving party.

Leku, Roku, Seiku, and Neku filled the room, and all were sitting intermixed, which surprised me. The current emergency obviously left little room for formalities or long standing rivalries, so sectors were seated next to each other with no rhyme or reason. On the far wall, the guards stood at attention, the head guard Logos in front smiling broadly as usual. A narrow passage cleared for our group as we pressed forward. I didn't think there would be enough room given the numbers already present, but somehow space was created.

Lianco moved regally through the crowd, a characteristic I had never before seen in him. People, or Beings I guess, nodded or bowed to him in deference to his authority. To me, he had always seemed the hotheaded, quick-thinking guy in charge, but here it was clear that his presence meant much more to the people of the Alliance than I had realized. As we walked toward the middle of the group on the bottom floor, I looked up and spotted one face I recognized. Gomer gave me a tiny wave from his place at the rail on the third tier. I followed his cue and replied with a subtle wave back.

The Council of Elders occupied their places on the perimeter of the open square, with each sector leader sitting directly in front of a wall of people. Laic took his Leku seat on the floor and the rest of us sat behind him. Lianco paced around in the open space between the four Elders. It was strange to see everyone gathered together. We had only encountered a few people here and there during our training, and occasionally passed one or two in the halls. Now, I could see the full power of the Alliance, and I felt completely insignificant in comparison to it. Dan and I were supposedly Rokenan warriors, but we really had no experience. Against a sea of Beings from the other sectors, we were just two college kids with a couple of days of training under our belts. How could we possibly make the difference they all expected us to?

"Greetings, friends." Lianco's voice rang out clearly as he addressed the massive crowd. "The Alliance has withstood the ages."

"Let it continue to be strong," replied the crowd.

Dan immediately shot a glance over to me. "Guess we weren't taught the secret password," he whispered. Alita whacked him hard on the arm she was sitting next to.

Lianco turned in a small circle as he spoke. When he faced our direction, I caught another glimpse of that golden chain around his neck, but before I could wonder any more about it, he continued his speech. "We have gathered here today to address the urgent issue that faces the Alliance. Our existence is being threatened. There are those who would like to see the end of our long union. We must work together to prepare for what is to come, for it will indeed affect us all."

I looked around, half-expecting whispered comments and questions to run through the crowd after Lianco's sweeping statement. But all of the attendees were completely silent, totally focused on the man in the center of the room, hanging on his every word. Lianco had obviously garnered a great deal of respect from the people of the Realm. I swelled up with pride from just knowing him like I did, and at being an integral part of this noble assembly.

"The Legends have just this day traveled to and returned from the Unknown," Lianco said as he turned to acknowledge the two of us. His statement earned us appreciative nods from the Council of Elders, and then the hum of whispers I had expected ran through the crowd. Following cues from our Masters, Dan and I each bowed our heads slightly to return respect and to show thanks. Such a compliment really deserved a bow from the waist, but that was impossible while seated on the floor.

"While in the Unknown, Zaria and Zoran were visited by the one man whom none of us hoped to see again: Serenu. He has somehow survived and we believe he is planning to retaliate. Their encounter with Serenu also revealed to us that Loki is alive, though we cannot be sure how powerful he remains. I am hereby placing the Alliance under a state of *concutio*.

"From this moment, no one is to travel alone at any time, for any reason. Should one of you come into contact with Serenu, you are hereby authorized to eliminate him by any means necessary. These are difficult times, but we must stand together to preserve our history." Lianco took a deep breath. "One final thing: if anyone should see Violet the Reiku, she is to be confined and brought to my office immediately for questioning. Be aware that she may be dangerous, so you have permission to use force to detain her, but do not injure her. It is imperative that we question her. You are dismissed. Go with care."

Everyone stood at attention as Lianco turned and exited the room the same way he had entered. I started to turn and follow, but Ariana motioned that we should wait. The Council of Elders stood and followed immediately behind Lianco, and then we fell in behind them, walking single file in the silence. As we got to the massive doors, I was relieved to hear quiet conversations start up in the crowded room. The silence had been unnerving

I was walking behind Ariana, watching her silvery hair swish back and forth, when I noticed four people fall in step on either side of me. Their presence startled me and I wondered if I should be concerned at the closeness of these strangers. I glanced over my shoulder at Dan, and could see a group around him as well. His expression told me he wasn't comfortable with it either—his concern was making that frown line between his eyebrows scrunch up. Given that we had been pointed out in the meeting as the Legends and that we were still in the middle of the crowd, I walked with my head held high, waiting for the right moment to find out who these people were. Testing myself and them, I veered right and left in the hallway once we had exited the doors, but they followed my movements with perfect precision. Fed up with the whole situation, I whirled around to face the four of them.

A short, pixie-faced blonde, a tall redhead, a chestnut-haired boy, and a boy with jet-black hair stared at the wall just over my head.

"Who are you people?" I demanded of the blonde, the

one who was closest to me. She refocused her turquoise eyes to look straight into mine.

"My name is Raine," she replied with a pleasant smile.

"Okay, Raine, why are the four of you tailing me?"

"We're your personal bodyguards," she quipped.

"My personal what?"

"Lianco assigned us to you, just as he assigned a group to your brother."

"Um, why?"

"In order to protect you from whatever is to come," she said. "Are you not pleased?"

"Pleased? It's not a matter of being pleased. Look, I don't have a problem with any of you. I just don't see why I need bodyguards."

"Forgive me for saying, Zaria, but you underestimate your importance to the Alliance."

"No doubt," I said with a sigh. "Fine, so you're my bodyguards. At least tell me the rest of your names."

"I'm Elianna," the redheaded girl said quietly.

"Teak," said the boy with brown hair.

"Nolan." The boy with jet-black hair spoke softly and never even looked my way.

"We are each from different sectors," Raine explained. "The variation of our powers will provide maximum protection."

I chuckled to myself. "Maximum protection, huh?"

Down the hall I could hear Dan's voice growing louder. From the sound of it, I could tell he was confronting his own bodyguards.

"Okay," I said, "now that we're all acquainted, tell me again who it was that assigned you to me?"

"Lianco," Raine answered quickly. Apparently, she was the spokesperson of the group.

"Well, no offense, but let's go find Lianco and see if we can undo his orders."

I tuned my senses to high alert as I ran to catch up with Lianco. I blew past Dan, who was waving his arms and talking loudly to his own foursome of followers. My posse kept my pace with ease, never breaking formation, never leaving my sides. We found Lianco in the Seiku sector, about to step into a chute.

"Lianco!" I cried as he dropped into the tunnel. To my amazement, his body nimbly floated back up the chute and he stepped out onto the floor beside me.

"What is it, Liz?" he asked. "I am in a hurry."

"Can you please get rid of these people?" I gestured to the four automatons behind me. "I don't need bodyguards."

"They are for your *protection*, Liz. I put them in place and I intend for them to stay."

"Lianco, I don't need protection and I sure don't need four people dogging my every step!" I said. "Neither does Dan! You haven't seen what we've learned. We're fully capable of defending ourselves."

"I saw what you learned from Alita, and I do not want another experience like your journey through the portal," Lianco said, in an exasperated tone. "You cannot walk around unguarded with my brother on the loose. If we lose you, we lose everything."

"Why?" I countered. "Why does everyone keep saying that? We're no more special than you are. In fact, you're probably more special! You're the leader of the whole Alliance! I saw how everyone looks up to you."

"But you and Dan are the last surviving Rokenan."

"So what?" He had tapped into the right nerve endings to make me very angry. "If we're so damn *special* and powerful, why don't you let us take care of ourselves? I don't want these four following me around all the time! It's obnoxious already, and they haven't even been with me ten minutes!"

The guard behind me stepped back just slightly and I could feel the invisible wall that now separated us. I didn't want them, and they knew it. *Great job, Liz,* I thought to myself, *way to stick your big foot in your mouth.*

"They have been instructed to be with you at all times," Lianco explained. "And they will fulfill that order. Raine has moved into your apartment to watch over you at night."

I looked back at Raine but her eyes were trained on the ground and her blonde hair covered her expression. "Moved in?" I asked quietly.

"She will be in the living area. She has her own cot. We especially cannot leave you unprotected at night," Lianco looked behind him anxiously. "You must stay inside and stay safe. Now, I really need to go."

I took a deep breath before speaking. "Okay, I'll deal with it. But no one, I mean *no one*, follows me into the bathroom." I swung around and looked straight at Raine for emphasis. A hint of a smile had appeared on her face as she glanced up to meet my eyes.

"Deal," she laughed. The others smiled appreciatively. I turned back to Lianco but he had already disappeared into the depths of the Seiku.

"Okay. We have a psycho on the loose and I've got the four of you for protection. What now?"

"You should probably rest," Raine replied. She was the spokesperson and now mommy, apparently.

"Fine. Let's go back to the apartment. I could use something to eat anyway. "

*   *   *

I dug my spoon into the container and pulled out a bite full of wonderful deliciousness.

"There is nothing like Ben & Jerry's cookie dough ice cream," I said through a mouthful. Raine and I were sitting on the couch, passing the container back and forth between us. Dan had stayed with us for a few minutes, but he was still fuming about being followed around, so he retreated to his room to sulk, slamming the door behind him. His 'live-in' guard was seated on the floor against the far wall, morosely watching us eat our snack. "Do you want some?" I called to him. He said nothing, just shook his head once and returned his attention to Dan's closed door.

Dan's main guy was far more intense than Raine. Aerik, as he was called, was gloomy-faced and apparently a bit over protective. He had long hair as dark as his moody scowl, and a permanent shoulder slouch that only added to his brooding aura. The rest of Dan's group included Eyla, whom I discovered was the twin of Elianna, a member of my personal guard. Then there was a brown-headed boy, Arpin, and a blonde girl, Lindle. All of them were polite and very quiet, just as my group was, but clearly Dan's rudeness had gotten things off to a rough start. He had not accepted his group, nor had he given them any instructions before disappearing into his room. So, they were all stuck sitting outside the apartment in the hallway with my guard. All except Aerik.

"So," I asked Raine, "how do you think this will all work out?"

"Do you mean with the Alliance?" she asked.

"Mm-hmm."

"Oh, we're all going to die," Raine said with utmost seriousness. I froze and looked at her in alarm. Her face broke into a smile. "I'm kidding!" she laughed. "I believe everything will be fine. We have been threatened before and we have always found a way to survive. Besides, you two are the greatest thing to happen to this place in a long time. You're the last of the Rokenan."

"Right, tell me something I don't know…" I mumbled.

"Come on, lighten up. You should be honored."

"That reminds me, you still haven't told me what sector you are," I mused, hoping to turn the attention away from me.

"I am Seiku," she smiled. "Elianna is Roku, Teak is Neku, and Nolan is Leku. As far as Dan's protectors go, Aerik is Leku, Eyla is Roku, Arpin is Neku, and Lindle is Seiku. I've known Lindle since we were little. She was always in my training classes and we've been good friends for a very long time." She had a faraway look for a moment before she held her hands out in Seiku fashion: hands together and palms up, like an open book. It was then that I noticed her Seiku mark. She motioned for me to put my hands out in the same way.

"Let's practice," she smiled.

Though Raine said nothing out loud, a spark lit from the air above her hands and a tiny flame appeared, hovering just inches above her palm. The flame danced in her hands. She was a Seiku with a lot of practice under her belt, so she was able to conjure the flame by speaking the command in her head. Challenged to do the same, I concentrated on my energies as I had been instructed and pulled the elements together.

"*Ignis.*"

Instantly, a flame appeared in my hands. I smiled as I realized that I had spoken the word in my mind, rather than out loud. Very pleased with myself, I showed off a little by rolling the flame around both sides of my hands before snuffing it out. From across the room, Aerik clapped a few slow beats, and smiled appreciatively. With Raine's encouragement, we moved on to practice with the other elements.

"Did the Master teach you about weather?" Raine, asked when we finished practicing the simple skills.

"You mean like storms and lightning and such?" I asked. Raine nodded. "Well, the Master didn't teach us, Alita did. So, I know how to conjure them, I mean I know *what* to do to conjure them, but our training was interrupted. I never got to actually use the skills."

"Oh, but you have to practice them so you can get better!" Raine said excitedly. "The weather spells are my favorite part about the Seiku sector! Creating tornadoes, storms, and hail…it's awesome!" Clearly she found weather exciting because her whole face lit up when she spoke of it. Her smiling eyes dimmed suddenly, and her mouth took on a slight pout as she looked around at the enclosed apartment. "But we can't do weather in here…"

"No, that would be a mess," I added, leaning over to take another bite of the melting ice cream. "Can you imagine the trouble we'd get into if we created a tornado or a thunder-storm in here? There's probably not enough magic available to fix that." I laughed and sank back into the sofa. "Guess we'll have to try it some other time."

Raine turned slightly toward me and continued in a quiet voice. "No, Zaria, you need all the practice you can get to defend yourself if the time comes that you have to. I am assigned to protect you, and this is a way I can help. First, we need to get out of here." I winced slightly at the 'Zaria' part, but she barreled through her speech without noticing. "I'm sure that Alita taught you how to bend the light to make yourself invisible, right?" I nodded in response. "Good. Well, what she didn't teach you is that there are two ways to make yourself invisible. When you bend the light around you, it's very easy for another Seiku to bend it back and see you instantly. The spell I'm going to teach you is less common, but it's more effective. It isn't hard, but it can backfire on you if you don't concentrate. You could end up with one arm still visible and then we'd have trouble putting you back together again. Understand?"

"Sure, I get it," I replied, uncertain about why she was going into all this detail. Lianco had made it clear that we should stay tucked away in our place. We weren't supposed to leave the apartment, but she was talking like we were going somewhere else to practice spells. My internal goody-two-shoes meter nagged at my conscience.

"Okay," Raine smiled. "Imagine pulling a curtain, or a blanket, over you from one side to the other. Pull it carefully, covering each part of your body. Keep thinking about wrapping it tightly around you, and making sure no body parts are left uncovered. Then, once you feel totally 'covered', say the right word and you'll disappear."

"What's the word?" I asked.

"Watch," she replied. "I'll demonstrate for you." She used one hand to draw the imaginary, invisible drape over herself. After about three seconds she said, *"invisibilis,"* and disappeared from view. I glanced over at Aerik, who was watching us carefully. Apparently he had seen Raine do this before because his face remained cemented in its usual scowl. I closed my eyes, centered my energies and concentrated hard on pulling my curtain closed around me.

"Invisibilis," I whispered. I didn't feel any different, but when I looked over, Aerik's eyes were practically bugging out of his head.

"I guess I did it," I whispered to Raine. "Now what?"

"We need to get out the door. Come with me," she whispered back. I could feel a slight breeze as her invisible form brushed past me. Than I felt her grab my equally invisible hand, tugging me after her.

Aerik stood and began walking with quick strides toward where we'd been sitting on the sofa. As silently as possible, we moved past him and bounded toward the door. Once we yanked it open, we began running full throttle. I listened for the sound of footsteps following as I was dragged along, but I couldn't hear anyone behind us. In no time, we were past the sentry guards, through the Film and onto the squishy grass of the college lawn.

"Reverse the motion and the curtain will be gone." Raine's voice floated near my left ear.

"Ugh," I said as I walked through a particularly soggy spot and splashed dirty water onto my now visible leg. In my jeans and t-shirt I was totally unprepared for the cold November night, but Raine took no notice. She made herself visible again and took a deep breath of the fresh Maryland air.

"Must've just rained," she remarked. "Then they won't mind some thunder." She smiled conspiratorially to herself.

The Film had spit us out on the edge of the Quad. I could see people coming out of the library at the other end of the large lawn, holding books above their heads. I wondered why, but my question was answered as I felt a few raindrops splatter on my head. A few drops turned into many, and pretty soon we were standing in the midst of a downpour. Trying to divert the water as I had learned in my Seiku training made no difference, for there were too many raindrops to keep away. In the midst of the downpour, I heard loud thunder booms and saw lightning flash in multiple places overhead. I saw that most of the students had run for cover.

"Raine!" I yelled over the noise. "I'm freezing and this storm is a little scary! Let's go find someplace dry!"

"Scary? This is your learning ground!" she yelled back. "Try a few for yourself. Point your arms at the sky and say *procella!*"

The storm responded with the loudest boom yet as my blonde guard threw her head back and screamed her magic at the heavens. Lightning snaked across the sky and I caught a glimpse of a lone figure on the library steps even as water poured over my face in streams. Raine laughed in delight at the tempest she'd created, exhilarated by its fury and oblivious to the cold. I had suddenly lost my desire to learn any new spells, and looked around for shelter. The mysterious figure on the steps was still there, standing motionless. Even from hundreds of feet away, I recognized the defiant stance and the thick black hair blowing across his face with the rain and wind. Lightning flashed again and illuminated his face. My suspicion was confirmed.

"*Raine,*" I screamed at her, "we have to go! *Now!*" I lunged for her arm to pull her back toward the Film.

"Why?" she yelled back, deftly extracting herself from my grasp. "This is *fun!*"

I looked back toward the steps for the figure, but he was gone. One of Raines' lightning bolts illuminated the Quad and I spotted him, moving swiftly toward us. He'd already closed half the distance between us and he wasn't alone. At least five people flanked him, and more were appearing by the second.

"We have to *go!*" I said as I bodily dragged Raine toward the Film, toward safety. I willed myself to resist the urge to look back at the evil force I knew was on its way.

Dan

"Go away!" I yelled at the insistent knocking on my door. Soon the knocking turned into pounding. Whoever it was had decided to keep at it until I showed, so I jerked the door open. Aerik had not said a word for the few minutes he had been knocking, and my calls of "I'm trying to sleep!" obviously hadn't meant anything to him.

"What do you want?" I yelled right in Aerik's face.

"It's your sister. She and Raine are gone," Aerik said softly.

"What?" I growled. "Speak up, man, what do you mean gone?"

"Well, they were just talking on the sofa, and then they got quiet, and then Raine disappeared, and then your sister disappeared, and—"

"Disappeared? Disappeared how?"

"I'm not sure. One moment they were sitting on the couch and the next, they weren't."

"*What?*"

"One minute they—"

"I heard you. An invisibility spell, you think?"

"I don't know," he shrugged. "I'm not Seiku."

"We have to find Lianco," I said hastily as I threw on my jeans. Aerik and I raced out the door, toward the Leku sector.

My other three bodyguards caught up with us about halfway there, and took up their positions.

"You three, spread out and find Liz!" I yelled, still running. "She's with Raine somewhere in this godforsaken place!"

With a short nod from Aerik, they melted away from my sides, each headed in a different direction. They would go to the furthest corners of the Alliance to look for my sister, of that I was sure. When the two of us reached Lianco, he was leaving a Leku training room. I toppled into him; his quick exit caught me off guard and I didn't have enough time to stop.

"What the...?" Lianco said angrily as he lifted himself off the floor and turned to glare at me. "What is the meaning of this?"

I started talking before I got up, so jumpy from the speed of our run and the adrenaline rush my fear had created, that I just babbled. "It's Liz, she's gone, Raine and her, both gone, we came as fast as we could. We need your—"

"Liz?" His face morphed from anger into concern within milliseconds and he reached out to pull me up. "Gone? Gone where?"

"I DON'T KNOW!" I shouted. "THAT'S WHY I CAME TO FIND YOU!"

"Calm down, Dan. I—"

"No! I will not calm down! My sister is out there somewhere and something bad could happen to her and I'm not there to protect her!"

"Everything okay?" Laic's face appeared in the doorway.

"No," Lianco replied. I was on the verge of tears and trying desperately to hold it together. This was no time for crying, this was time for action, and I was impatient to get moving again. But where should we go?

"We don't have time to talk! We need to find Liz immediately," Lianco said with authority. His face went still as he concentrated hard, using that inside his head speaking stuff that he and some of the others did. No doubt he was mobilizing his troops—anyone and everyone who could help us find Liz.

"You two! Follow me," Lianco commanded.

I fell into step behind him with Aerik at my side.

*   *   *

The massive doors flew open as we raced into the Roku sector. The place was completely deserted, save for Master Skren who was seated in a meditative pose in the middle of the mats.

"Skren?" Lianco called. "We need your help, and we are in a hurry."

With trance-like slowness, Skren rose to his feet. Then, almost like some old kung-fu movie, he took a few steps and vaulted himself onto the second floor in a single leap.

"Whoa," I exclaimed. "I gotta learn how to do that."

Unable to duplicate the Master's feat, Lianco and I used the *ventus* spell to lift ourselves to the second floor to join him.

"Now, Dan," Lianco said patronizingly, "if there is to be

a battle, you are likely to be put in a situation where you need protection. We need you to be fully armed."

"Fully armed, huh? Does that mean I have to wear the whole outfit?"

"What do you mean 'the whole outfit'?"

"Gauntlets, chainmail, you know, battle armor…" I said wearily.

Lianco laughed roughly. "No…ordinary armor would only hinder your other skills. You simply need a weapon and your nanocloth," he replied patiently.

"Oh, oh yeah. Right."

"So," Master Skren asked, "which weapon do you feel most comfortable with? Sword? Saber? Scythe?"

"Mace? Mallet?" Lianco added.

"Um…I…ah…" I looked around at the weapons leaning against the wall. I couldn't decide. They were all wickedly sharp, and somehow, fantastically appealing. "I can't decide," I admitted sheepishly.

"Try this one," Master Skren said, and handed me a scimitar. The weapon was beautiful. The scimitar blade was longer and thinner than the average sword, and formed a deadly curve at the end. The slim, silver blade shone brightly even in the shadowy weapons room. I suddenly realized it was perfect. It felt perfect. I smiled down at it, thinking how similar this was to the warrior movies I had seen, and turned the blade around in my hand. The handle was exquisite, silver and royal blue with flecks of gold. The size fit my hand just right. The blue matched my portal magic, too, which made me smile to myself.

I glanced up to see Master Skren smiling back at me, pleased that he'd suggested a weapon I obviously liked.

"It's perfect. I'll take it."

A low rumble sounded through the sector, slightly shaking the ground beneath my feet.

"What was that?" I asked, confused. "I thought outside weather and stuff like that couldn't affect the Alliance."

"It can't…" Lianco looked seriously worried. "At least, the usual kinds of weather can't."

"Then there's something *unusual* going on. C'mon, we have to find Liz," I said, grabbing the scimitar's sheath from Skren and fastening it to my jeans. I groaned a little as I realized that jeans and a t-shirt would not be the best attire for a fight. Luckily, Skren was one step ahead of me.

"Put this on," he said as he tossed a nanocloth shirt at me. I could hear Skren and Lianco whispering beside me as I stripped off my thin t-shirt and struggled into the snug, protective garment.

"Let's go!" I said impatiently as soon as the nanocloth was on.

"Good luck!" Master Skren called after us, but Lianco, Aerik and I were too far away to call back.

Forty-Seven

Liz

We pushed through the Film with the threatening group only seconds behind us. Raine was still giggling like a four-year-old in her soaked clothes, almost as if she was drunk. Fearing the group would burst through and catch up to us any second, I frantically turned back and forth, searching for a familiar face among the guards. I didn't see Logos, but the rest of them were cautiously watching me and I had no time left.

"Listen up!" I yelled at the guards. "You have to close the Film right now! Break it, turn off the power, lock it, do whatever it is you do to make sure no one can go in or out! Something is about to come—"

They were all staring at me intently, but looked confused by my rapid-fire commands. They were not used to responding quickly to new authority. Their brains didn't work as fast as even the dumbest humans. I didn't get a chance to explain before the person I feared most burst through the Film, his menacing ranks not far behind him.

The long, wavy hair, eyes black as night; my whole body shook with fear. His lips turned up in a thin smile, then he grinned larger as he realized his advantage in the room. His teeth were so unnaturally white they were almost blinding. So I ran, faster than ever before, and pulled Raine along with me.

Muffled shrieks echoed in the halls around me, and I sent

out a prayer to whoever watched over those guards to keep them safe in their next life. Silence resumed, and the sound of my feet and Raine's running for our lives were the only things I heard. I careened around a corner and slammed into Eyla, one of Dan's guards.

"Zaria!" She exclaimed. She looked extremely relieved, then very confused when she saw Raine and I were both dripping wet. "Were you two *outside?*"

"*Shh!* There's no time to talk!" I said as forcefully as I could in a whisper. I could hear the sounds of running coming closer.

"Don't you know?" Eyla looked shocked. "Raine can't go outside. Not in this kind of weather, especially. The rain is like a drug to her, she loses all sense of reason; no one knows why. It must be her namesake, since she's the only one affected that way."

I was slightly puzzled, but Eyla just shrugged and raised her hand. The sound that ensued was so loud that I couldn't believe it came from human skin. Raine's cheek had a big red handprint on it and she glared up at Eyla, obviously herself again.

"*What the hell?*" Raine said angrily.

"Look at you!" Eyla whisper-yelled. Raine looked down at her soaked clothes and over at mine, and her embarrassment was obvious.

"I went out in the rain, didn't I?" she asked quietly.

"Look, we can have an intervention later," I hissed. "Serenu has broken through the Film. He's in the Alliance and he's not alone."

"Oh my god…" Eyla panicked. The footsteps I'd heard were getting closer, and by the sound of them, there was quite a group coming our way. Serenu was definitely not alone. "Go," she said, pushing us down the hallway.

"But—"

"Go! I'll handle this and meet up with you later," she said, looking determined.

"We can't leave you alone!" I cried.

"Go now! Don't argue!" Eyla reached to the belt around her waist and grabbed a small object the size of a lighter. At her touch, the silver rectangle morphed itself, growing, changing and unfolding into a broadsword. Eyla grinned at my stunned expression. "New technology. Now go. I'll catch up."

She turned to bravely face the coming attack as now Raine took the lead and pulled me down the hallway. My eyes brimmed with tears that were swiftly blown away by our speed. Eyla didn't have a chance, and she took a stand for me anyway.

So we ran. I wasn't positive what Raine's intentions were, but I had a pretty good idea that we were looking for Dan, since the apartment was the first place she checked. We looked in the Seiku and Neku sectors, both of which were deserted with the exception of a few older golems in Neku. We were on our way to Leku when I spotted movement at the end of the hallway. Raine and I flattened ourselves against the wall as best we could. There was nowhere to hide. I willed myself to blend in with the stone, an impossible task. I had just decided to try the invisibility spell when I took another look down the hallway and a torch illuminated a length of long, silvery hair.

"Ariana!" I cried, running for her.

"Where in the world have you been?" she said through tears. "And why are you wet?"

"Serenu's here," I said with a catch in my voice.

"Here? *Inside?*"

"Yes. He's in the Alliance, and he has a small army with him."

Running figures rounded the corner and Raine quickly sent a bolt of fire flashing across the ceiling for illumination purposes.

"Dan!" I screamed. I threw myself toward my brother, and hugged him tightly, unwilling to let go.

"You're soaked. Where were you?" he said roughly.

"Doesn't matter right now. Serenu's here, and he's killing everyone in his path."

Lianco grabbed my shoulder and locked his eyes with mine.

"He is here? In the Alliance?"

I nodded. "He's not alone, either." Lianco looked far away for a moment, no doubt searching the Alliance with his mind for signs of his brother.

"We need to get Serenu out of here," Lianco said. "We are losing people way too fast."

"He's not going to just walk out. How are we supposed to get him to leave?" Ariana asked quietly.

"We will have to be the bait. We must get out of the Alliance and go to human soil to fight. But we have to get close enough to Serenu that he will sense us and follow us

there. He would not turn down a chance to fight me."
Lianco turned to Dan and I. "Can you two have a portal
ready when they get close?"

"Absolutely," we replied in unison.

"Excellent. He is passing Seiku and coming fast." Lianco
grimaced and shook his head.

Dan and I began forming our portal, his ball of blue light
and my ball of yellow growing bigger and brighter.

"Getting closer…" Lianco warned.

Still our lights grew.

"Closer…"

We pushed our hands to the wall.

"Come on…"

The light spread quickly and the portal appeared in total,
as if it sensed our urgency. We left our hands on the wall to
hold the portal open as long as possible. I could hear echoes
of shouting down the corridor.

"Now!" Lianco yelled. Ariana and Raine dove through
the doorway as Serenu and his followers rounded the corner.
Lianco, Dan and I dodged the lightning bullets they shot at
us as we jumped through the green wall, which dissipated
behind us. As we did, I heard a short scream.

"Oh my gosh. Where are we?" I asked. Bright lights
shone down on us and the rain, which had finally let up to a
fine mist, sparkled around us. I rubbed my eyes and tried to
make sense of what I saw. One very startled boy was sprawled
on the ground in front of us and Ariana was brushing herself
off next to him. Fourteen other boys in uniforms gaped at us
from various positions on the field.

"What the hell?" I heard the one closest to me say.

A lone soccer ball flew toward us and Dan snagged it deftly out of the air. The player who had kicked it stood defiantly for a moment, then his smug expression faded into fear and disbelief. With expert skill, Dan punted the ball back, hitting the still open-mouthed boy right in the chest.

Lianco

A soccer field. We had emerged right in the middle of the soccer team's evening practice and scared the freshman goalie out of his mind. The weather was still out of control—lightning flashed everywhere and thunder boomed overhead, but at least the rain had stopped. Liz looked to me with the obvious question.

"What do we do now?" she whispered. "These guys can't stay here if Serenu is following us."

I strode up beside her, drew myself up to full height, and took on an air of authority. "A tornado warning has been issued for this area. You are all asked to return to your dorms at this time," I called across the field.

"Dude!" said the goalie, who was still lying on the ground from shock. "You guys came out of *nowhere!*"

"I am serious, boys. Everyone needs to go! Now!"

Begrudgingly, and not without a few dirty looks that were barely illuminated in the darkness, the team grabbed their gear and jogged toward the main part of the campus.

"A soccer field?" Dan asked Liz sarcastically. "Seriously?"

"I was nervous!" she defended.

"Listen," I interjected, fearful that our pursuers would be on us immediately. "We do not have time to argue!"

I heard a soft humming from the other side of the field

and whipped around to face it. The others saw my expression and turned to face what was coming. A portal appeared and three figures walked out.

"You weren't going to start without us, were you?" Alita yelled from across the field. She jogged toward us with Darien and Orion not far behind her.

"No, I think they were waiting for me," came a voice from behind us. A voice I knew all too well.

Illuminated by the field lights, a solitary figure was seated atop the soccer goal. Serenu sat on the cross bar, his legs lazily swinging back and forth.

"Hello brother," he said with a contemptuous smirk. "Miss me?" He paced across the top of the goal, not ten feet from us, stepping lazily along the thin metal beam. "You are weak, Lianco. You and your 'warriors' make this too easy. Easy to fool, easy to track, easy to humiliate."

The very sight of him made me angry. On instinct, I balled my hands into fists.

"Watch your temper, brother," he smiled. "We wouldn't want anyone to get hurt." After he spoke, he raised his chin to signal behind me.

I turned slowly, afraid of what I was about to see. Alita and Orion were on their knees in the grass, with their arms above their heads. I could sense their powers had been disabled. Behind them stood Violet and Darien, weapons drawn, ready to strike and kill.

Momentarily, I was puzzled. Why would Darien be holding a weapon on one of my people? I let it go and turned back to my brother.

"What do you want?" I growled at Serenu.

"I just want to have the satisfaction of watching you die before I have the pleasure of erasing all of you forever," he said in a smug voice. "Before I erase the whole of the Alliance from the Book and rewrite things to fit my standards."

"Does that mean Darien is one of *them*?" Liz whispered to me from the side of her mouth.

At that moment, Darien stood over Orion, longsword poised to strike through his supposed comrade's throat. *How could he have betrayed us*? I thought angrily.

"Darien, how could this be?" I yelled. "Do you know whom you serve?" He said nothing in return, simply stared through me as if I did not exist.

"I had to have someone who knew you well, brother," Serenu chuckled. "And Darien was just *so* eager to help."

"What did you do to him?" Ariana spoke up for the first time. Serenu looked shocked to hear her voice again, after what had happened between them. He was obviously impacted by the venom that laced her question. He had not seen her in her new form, but he would have recognized her voice anywhere.

"I did absolutely nothing to him."

"*Liar.*" Ariana's voice was hard, unforgiving. "Don't think I don't know what you're capable of."

I stole a glance over at Darien but he still would not meet my gaze. Everyone else did, however. Violet glared back with taunting eyes, daring me to do something that would permit her to drive her sword straight through Alita. My dear Alita, facing death, but trying desperately to catch the eye of the man who would decide her fate, the man she loved. Orion simply watched me. He had accepted his role as my protector long ago, and he knew that might require his death one day. His look was one of respect and even goodbye. I had few cards to play and one wrong turn would mean the death of two very dear friends...if not the death of all of us.

"Here's what we'll do," Serenu said, pacing back and forth on the narrow top of the soccer goal. "You give me the Rokenan twins over there, and you and everyone else can go free." He smiled thinly. "Or, you can try to resist handing them over, in which case we would just have to slaughter every one of you."

"You would allow her to kill the woman you love?" I pointed at Violet and Alita.

"The woman I love?" he laughed. "Oh, you mean the woman who *ruined me*?" He shouted the last part for Alita's benefit. Her head sagged, only to be jerked up again roughly by Violet.

"How can you blame her for your mistakes, for your practicing the Dark magic? It is your own fault you were denied acceptance into our world. How can you just let her die?"

"How can you just let her die?" he mimicked. "The same way I've let go of everyone else in my life. Mother never wanted me. She got *you*, the perfect son, the golden child. She didn't care anything about me," he spat.

"This is not about her!"

"It's always been about her! She hated me and loved you!

This is what we always get back to! Now, hand over the Rokenan."

Ariana, I need you to stall, I sent at her. She stepped up to the front of our little group, perfectly at ease facing her old childhood friend-turned-killer, and began to speak.

Liz, don't move or look at me.

She stiffened beside me, unused to having a voice speak to her inside her head. But to her credit, her face gave nothing away.

I need you to be ready to fight. If you can do that, signal by shifting your weight slightly. Once I saw that she had heard me, I sent instructions. *On my signal, blast a lightning bolt into Violet and help Alita get to cover. She is temporarily powerless, so you will be her protection.*

Once again, Liz shifted her weight to signal that she had understood. I quickly focused on Ariana, long enough to see that she was still engaged in an argument with Serenu, but his attention was wavering. His eyes narrowed and started to scan our group. He was looking for movement and strategy. I did not have much time.

I'll have Dan do the same with a fire attack on Darien. Once they recover, you will probably have to face them hand to hand. Don't look back. Don't worry about us. Just keep moving and stay focused.

I finished giving Dan his instructions and began the countdown in everyone's head.

3…2…1

"Fulmen!" "Ignis!"

Lightning and fire shot out of the twins' fingertips as they ran to face their opponents. Serenu was momentarily stunned, and Raine and I were on him in seconds.

"*Aqua!*"

"*Terra!*"

"*Ignis!*"

"*Aere!*"

A host of elements flew around Serenu as we attacked and he counterattacked our magical abilities. It was obvious he had become much stronger since we last saw him. Although we fought to keep as many elements around him as possible to keep him distracted, the spells we sent began to disappear faster than we could keep them coming. Our ball of elements was dissipating, when it was gone we would be exposed to the worst of his Dark magic. Ariana hung back, knowing that her Roku would not help in a Seiku battle.

"*Fulmen!*" Serenu thundered, and a bolt of black lightning slammed into Raine, sending her flying across the field. Triumphantly, Serenu looked down at me and smiled.

Forty-Nine

Liz

The force of my lightning sent Violet flying as I rushed to Alita's side and helped her rise.

"Make a portal!" I huffed.

"I can't, at least for a moment. Plus, I would never leave!" she argued.

"Fine! At least hide!"

She and a freed Orion shuffled over to the practice field's bleachers, seeking whatever cover they could find while they recovered their abilities. Dan and I turned to face our opponents.

"So!" Violet yelled from where she had landed on her butt a few meters away. "You're back for more! I warned you this wouldn't be fun!"

In a flurry of skill, she sent out four different attacks almost simultaneously that left me scrambling to dodge and counter. Lucky for Dan, he had a weapon, a wicked looking scimitar which he was using to fend off Darien and his daggers. Violet had her magic and the ugly longsword she had been holding on Alita. I only had my magic and a tragic shortage of experience.

"So," I heard Dan say tauntingly, "you were never really *protecting* Lianco, were you Darien?" He was breathing hard. "You were only a lousy spy for that bastard."

With two quick parries and a deft move even I didn't know, Dan had Darien on his knees. Darien's daggers lay strewn across the grass. Violet sensed my distraction and seized the moment to charge at me with her longsword. I ducked to the side at the last minute and narrowly avoided an arm removal, but the sharp pain in my shoulder and liquid on my arm told me I wasn't untouched.

"Liz!" Dan called out sharply from where he had subdued Darien and paralyzed his abilities. "Here." I whipped my head around just in time to catch his blade in midair. The scimitar was lighter than it appeared. The handle was easy to grip and the weapon felt surprisingly good in my hand. Violet narrowed her eyes as she realized her odds had changed a bit. Her chances of a quick defeat had evaporated into the misty air. Back and forth we went, thrusting and dodging with quick, deft strokes that left me breathless and a little off-balance. Although I absolutely loathed Violet, I had to admire her talent in a fight. Suddenly, there was a loud thud on the grass beside me. A blackened, slightly charred Raine lay motionless in the grass.

"Oh my god," I breathed, as I looked down at her lifeless body.

I heard the whizzing of the blade before I saw it, but the shock of seeing Raine's limp body had dulled my reactions. I couldn't move fast enough and the tip of Violet's blade grazed my left cheek. I instantly felt the sticky blood on my face.

"Poor Liz, you never were quite fast enough," she chided in that voice I despised with a passion. She was referring to my lack of athletic prowess in high school, and possibly my social shortcomings as well. I had endured Violet/Brooke's insults and teasing for years, and suddenly everything boiled to the surface.

With the scimitar held high, I rushed at her with a fury she obviously didn't expect. I forced her back with every blow, driven by the anger I had held in for so many years. All the nicknames, insults, and snide comments I'd endured filled me with raw power. That power, combined with my recent Rokenan training, gave me the edge I needed. Against that amount of wrath, Violet didn't stand a chance.

"Nicely done," Dan congratulated me, staring condescendingly at a kneeling, subdued Violet. Remembering my training with Laic, I concentrated on my body and successfully healed the few wounds I'd suffered, leaving tiny, white scars behind. We turned to watch the scene unfolding before us, and Alita and Orion crept out from under the bleachers to stand with us.

"We have to help them," Alita said.

"We have to help them," Violet mimicked, earning herself a hard slap across the face from Alita.

"Zip it, mini me," she growled.

"Who the hell do you think you are?" Violet countered.

"That's *Alita*," I said sweetly. Dan laughed and Violet went absolutely silent. Now that she was subdued, I had the freedom to say Alita's name as many times as I wanted, and there was nothing Violet could do to stop me.

"We'll take over from here," Alita said. She and Orion took over as the guards for their former jailers, placing their fingers on the pressure points of the prisoners' necks to render their skills useless. Dan and I strode toward Lianco, determined to use whatever force we could to help. Even from a distance I could see Serenu's body shaking with anger. Without warning, he lunged toward Ariana, and a bolt of lightning flashed from beside me, headed straight for the one person who didn't need provoking.

"Oh, no," I groaned.

Lianco

"You don't even know the meaning of *pain!*" Ariana spat. "You don't know what it's like to wake up one day and not look like yourself! To look in the mirror and wonder who's looking back! My whole body changed thanks to *you!* My hair, my eyes, my skin...*all* of me is different because of your wounded *pride!*"

Serenu said nothing. He only stared at her as she yelled. But the longer she went on, the more his anger grew. He had never been good at keeping his temper and this was a real test for him. I watched as his hands balled into fists and his body began to quiver.

"You screwed me over!" Ariana continued. "You were my best friend and you hurt me, and then you didn't even have the decency to stay with me! You *ran!* As if I didn't even *matter* to you!"

In one swift movement, Serenu leapt from his position near the goal and landed not two feet from the now hysterical Ariana. Before I could even react, a bolt of lightning smashed into Serenu's chest, and he was thrown backward twenty feet. He slammed into the soccer net, and fell limp on the wet ground. Shocked, I looked at Dan, whose face was a mix of emotions. He was astonished at his ability, afraid of the possible repercussions, and weary of trying so hard to be brave. I nodded to encourage him and turned my attention back to Serenu.

How he stood up after that blast I do not know. But he did, and he careened drunkenly toward Dan, who was still a bit shell shocked. Serenu raised his hand and fired, but Liz was faster. She deflected his lightning bolts and sent a number of her own. Dan fired back weakly, but by then, I had stepped forward to blast Serenu from behind.

Nature became a factor in the fight as the storm that Raine had started during her lesson with Liz flared up again. A dense rain poured down on everyone, seriously affecting our visibility. Lightning flashed mightily across the sky, smashed into one of the giant field lights, and sent sparks flying everywhere.

"I *will* rewrite history!" Serenu managed to yell over the storm's fury.

A portal opened in the air above Serenu and the Book dropped right down into his hands. As if on cue, white-hot lightning shot out from each of us, every bolt amplified by the weather. Liz, Dan, and I reached our fingers toward him, striking him simultaneously. The Book exploded out of his hands, his body stiffened and arched backward, and then slumped sideways onto the grass. Without a thought to her safety, Liz ran forward to retrieve the precious Book. She retreated to Alita's side, close enough to reengage if the fight should continue, but far enough away to guard the Book.

"Is he...?" Ariana asked quietly. I could hardly hear her through the pouring rain.

"Dead?" I finished. She nodded. "I don't know."

I stared at the limp form of my half brother lying in the grass. He had betrayed us all, yet what I felt for him was only pity. Well, that along with a certain disgust at what he had allowed himself to become.

Things happened so fast after that. Violet broke free from Alita's grip and sent three simultaneous bolts of lightning into the remaining stadium lights, plunging us all into darkness. There was a lot of shouting as we tried to find each other by sending out *ignis* spells. We were frantic to recapture Violet. Somehow, in the chaos, she made her way to Serenu's side. The next lightning flash illuminated the soccer field and its occupants. Violet was gone, and so was Serenu's body.

Dan

"Do you think she took him with her?" I asked Liz as we walked alone for the first time in a while. Darien's trial had just ended and we were looking forward to some unstructured time of rest and relaxation. During the trial proceedings, it was revealed that Darien's loyalty had been compromised. He had been forced into Serenu's service because of threats on his wife and parents. Lianco was relieved to know the truth. And, in his usual gracious understanding way, Lianco held no grudge against Darien. In fact, Darien was returned to service and granted a full pardon.

"Yeah, I think she took his body," Liz said softly. "Do you think he's dead?"

"I don't know. Could be," I replied.

Five days had passed since that night on the soccer field, and Liz was finally getting around to talking about it. She never failed to amaze me with how long she could mull over something before she was ready to discuss it. The rest of us had already gone over it at length and found ways to go back to our daily routines.

Alita resumed teaching her classes. Overall, she spoke very little about the incident, but we all knew she was sensitive about the subject. None of us wanted to exacerbate the pain by pushing her too much. Orion never left Lianco's side, silently punishing himself for not being a better protector and friend. Raine lay motionless in the intensive care wing of Leku with such severe burns that Laic told us she would take months to heal. Everyone was starting to move on, and the rest of the Alliance was struggling to do the same.

We walked slowly to our next destination, dragging our feet in order to escape the reality we were approaching. When we reached the funeral location, Liz immediately found Elianna in the crowd and went to comfort her. She wrapped her arms around the taller girl, and Elianna sobbed softly into Liz's shoulder. I stayed where I was, gravely surveying the scene around me. The room was not as splendid as the rest of the Alliance, though it was enormous and very well lit. The walls were a sandy-colored stone, something Liz would probably know the name of, and stone benches were arranged in two neat rows that filled the room. The hundreds of mourners, dressed in the traditional white, huddled on the benches in groups, talking softly and watching the far end of the room solemnly. Everyone, including Liz and myself, wore white as instructed. White symbolized purity, and tradition held that purity was to be celebrated at Alliance memorial services. Purity of heart, mind, and spirit.

The people on benches were looking at the end of the room to where a channel no more than five feet across had been cut into the wall of stone. Crystal clear water ran through the opening. The surface of the water refracted the light and sent white reflections dancing across everyone's faces. Some of the Alliance members helped lift the shrouded bodies of their fallen comrades into the water, where they drifted past tearful family members who lined the channel. All eyes watched until the body floated out of sight. People from each of the sectors were present to remember the loved ones that were lost. Over five hundred Beings had perished in the fight with Serenu and his demon ranks, nearly one-fourth of the actively fighting Alliance members.

"It's very sad, isn't it?" Ariana's soft voice spoke beside me. She looked radiant in a simple, white dress that perfectly set off her hair.

"Yes, it is," I murmured. "But it's beautiful too. What do you call this place?"

"This is the Hall of Mourning," she smiled sadly. "We gather here to honor the dead and usher them into the next life. That river," she pointed to the channel, "is called Omi. It is the only one of its kind in the Alliance. Nothing else like it exists here in this Realm. We do not know where the Omi begins or ends, only that it passes through that opening, and takes our fallen onto their next journey."

A few moments of silence passed, and then Lianco appeared beside Ariana, looking sharp in a tailored white suit. He smiled and reached into his pocket, and pulled out a closed fist.

"Well done, Zoran," he said. "Well done. You risked your life for the Alliance and your bravery and honor in battle will long be remembered. As a symbol of your place in our Realm, I would like to give you this emblem of the Alliance." He opened his hand to reveal a shiny, gold medallion. Each sector's mark was etched onto its surface, and they gleamed in the light. Lianco smiled as he draped the chain over my head, and gently squeezed my forearm, before making his way toward Liz. My sister and Elianna were still enveloped in a tight hug, and Liz dried her eyes quickly when Lianco tapped on her shoulder. I watched as she received the same speech, and saw her face light up when Lianco produced her medallion. She beamed as he put the medallion over her head, and caught my gaze as he moved away into the crowd to comfort the other mourning families.

Ariana followed my eyes, and smiled at the scene. Her smile became broader, almost wistful, until she was practically grinning.

"Ariana," I teased, "we are at a funeral. No smiling allowed."

She grinned even bigger.

"What is it?" I asked.

"Everything is finally working out," she sighed. "You two are alive and well, Darien is free, Serenu is gone, and Lianco and I…"

Liz had received a few congratulations from those around her but was making her way toward us.

"What was that about you and Lianco?" she asked casually. Ariana looked at her with wide eyes, surprised that she had heard her so easily. "Hey, I'm Rokenan," Liz said as she held up her medallion. "What can I say?"

"Well," Ariana smiled, "Lianco will be frustrated that I said anything before he got a chance to tell you…" She paused for a long moment, and then whispered, "We're engaged!" Liz broke out into finger-tip applause, and I stood openmouthed like a fool. A flicker of a frown crossed Ariana's features as she said, "At least, it's what you two would call being engaged."

"That's fantastic!" Liz rejoiced. "I'm so happy for you!"

I recovered and gave my congratulations as well, then nudged Liz to indicate I was ready to leave. We didn't get a chance to before Ariana encouraged (pushed) us closer to the Omi, to pay our respects and share in wishing better journeys to the fallen. Even I got caught up in the mood and visited with as many family members as I could. My white button down grew moist from the tears of fellow Alliance members, and I could tell Liz's dress was the same way, even more so thanks to some of her own tears. It was a long time before we made our way back toward the entrance.

"That is such a beautiful way for their loved ones to be remembered," Liz commented as we walked out the way we had come in. She dabbed at her eyes and succeeded in smearing the mascara that had run down her cheek. "Aw, hell," she complained as she wiped the black off of her fingers.

"So what now?" I asked. Our footsteps echoed in the corridor and rang in my ears.

"No idea," Liz quipped.

"Yeah, me either."

Liz paused, and then looked at me for a long moment. A trace of a smile pushed its way across her face. "Race you back to the apartment!" Liz laughed, as she hiked up her dress and broke into a full run. I caught up with her easily, pushing the air under my feet to give myself an extra boost of speed.

Sarah Freese

"No Seiku!!" Liz shrieked as I came even with her. Her curly dark hair streamed behind her. We were laughing so hard as we reached our door, each of us trying to push the other out of the way to be the first inside. Neither of us won; instead, we sank to the floor of the corridor laughing and poking each other.

"No offense, Zaria, but you run like a girl," I said.

"That's okay, Zoran. You run like a golem."

We laughed simultaneously, admiring our new medallions as we regained our breath.

"Quite a semester," she said quietly.

"Tell me about it…." I replied.

A few moments of enjoyable silence passed.

"I love you, Dan."

"Back at you, sis."

We hugged this time for real.

"So much for our freshman year at college."

260

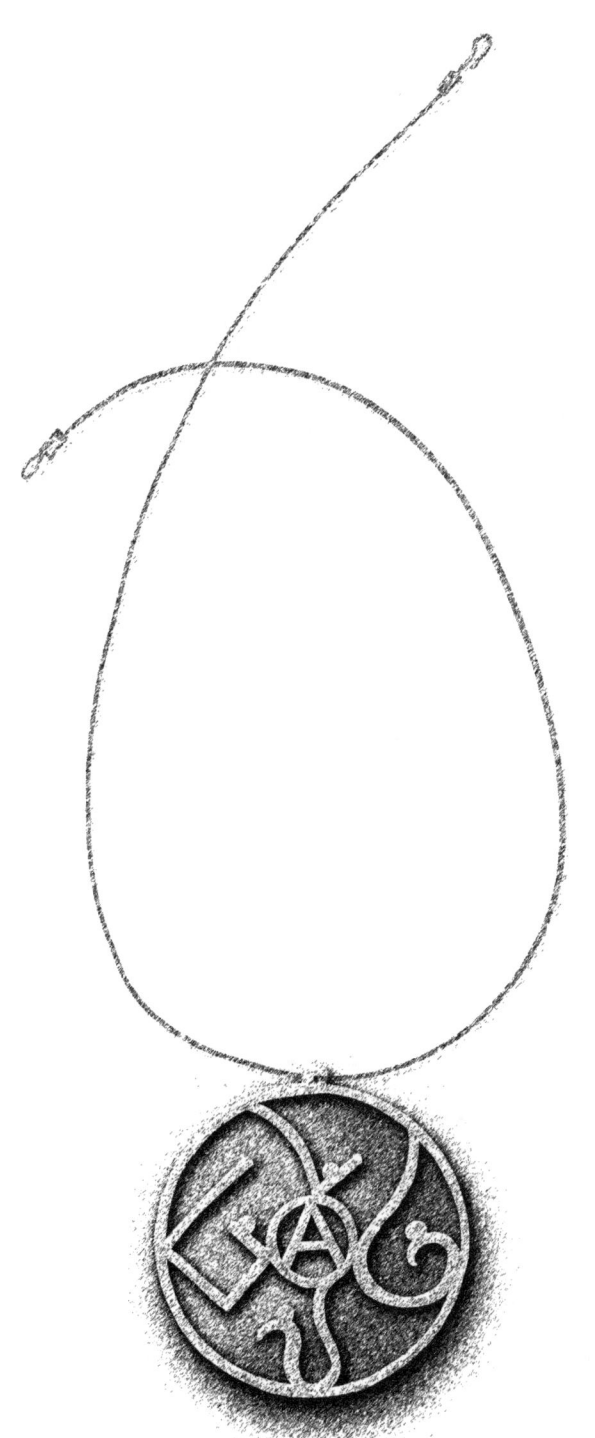

Acknowledgements

This project would not have been possible without the help of some very important people:

First of all, thank you to my family. Thank you, Dad, for the resident author's advice I needed and for modeling the kind of drive and perseverance that inspired me to write. Bless you Mom, for your sympathy, patience, advice, love, and extraordinary editing abilities. And, of course, kudos to my sister, whose witty sarcasm and daily antics provided a basis for one of the most important characters. You all kept me going on this project and refused to let me give up, and I appreciate your support so much.

My thanks to Dr. Skipper Gholston for his advice on the biological details. I tried to keep it close to reality, G.

Also, I couldn't have done this without my friends. You guys are amazing and I felt you by my side every step of the way. Without your pushes and your encouragement this book might never have been finished.

Lastly, I have to thank the staff of the local Borders. Their delicious bagels and endless hot chocolate gave nourishment and energy to the author on many occasions. They put up with me and my notebooks twice a week for months.

About the Author

Sarah Freese lives in Johns Creek, Georgia, with her parents, sister, and her two favorite dogs. She is a senior at Northview High School, where she is active in clubs and charity work. Sarah will attend a large southeastern university in the fall.

Sarah has always been a voracious reader and her joy in books stimulated a desire to author her own work. She started writing short stories and poems at an early age, and has had several poems published in school literary magazines and nationwide poetry collections. *The Alliance* is her first novel.

www.ingramcontent.com/pod-product-compliance
Lightning Source LLC
Chambersburg PA
CBHW061559170626
46811CB00001B/260